"You're putting in quite a lot of effort to find out about me. I'm not sure you even need me anymore." He let the humor he felt seep into his tone.

She rolled her eyes, but her smile remained, bright and beautiful. "You flatter me, Ken. It's my job to know as much as I can about you. I do the same thing with all my interview subjects."

Draining his smoothie, he looked into her eyes. "Really. How many of your subjects have you gone running with? Or done martial arts with?"

She blinked, then her gaze fled from his. "None. You're the first."

He adjusted his expression, hoping to indicate how he felt about the double meaning of her words.

Her eyes grew wide, and she sat straight up in her chair as the realization hit her. She hit the button on her phone to cease the recording. "Wait. I didn't mean it like that. I meant… Well, you know what I meant." She looked flustered, even a bit embarrassed.

It was a big change from the put-together, confident woman he'd come to know, but parts of him enjoyed seeing her a bit off her game. "However you meant it, I'm not against being y

Dear Reader,

Thank you so much for picking up *Tempo of Love*. This is the last title in my Gentlemen of Queen City series; at least, that's the plan. It's bittersweet for me to leave the gents behind, but I truly hope you've enjoyed the ride. Ken and Nona's relationship is full of ups and downs, curves and detours—will they make it to the end of the road together? Turn the page and find out!

All the best,

Kianna

Tempo of Love

Kianna Alexander

HHARLEQUIN® KIMANI™ ROMANCE

ISBN-13: 978-0-373-86504-8

Tempo of Love

Printed in U.S.A.

Kianna Alexander, like any good Southern belle, wears many hats: loving wife, doting mama, advice-dispensing sister and gabbing girlfriend. She's a voracious reader, an amateur seamstress and occasional painter in oils. Chocolate, American history, sweet tea and Idris Elba are a few of her favorite things. A native of the Tar Heel state, Kianna still lives there with her husband, two kids and a collection of well-loved vintage '80s Barbie dolls.

Books by Kianna Alexander

Harlequin Kimani Romance

This Tender Melody
Every Beat of My Heart
A Sultry Love Song
Tempo of Love

Visit the Author Profile page
at Harlequin.com for more titles.

For Kaia. I love you deeply…
except when you're critiquing me. JK. Never change.

Acknowledgments

Many thanks to Jennifer C, my assistant, and the members of Kianna's Royal Kourt street team. I appreciate all your hard work. My thanks also goes to Priscilla Johnson, who is a great friend and an invaluable supporter. To my Destin Divas: stay awesome. Thanks also to LaSheera Lee, LaShaunda Hoffman, Ronald Headen, Anya Alsobrook and the book clubs who support me.

You all rock!

Chapter 1

"Yo! Nona!"

Nona Gregory heard her name being called but didn't bother looking up from her computer screen. She was typing, fast and furious, determined to get the latest draft of her article on her boss's desk by the end of the day. Given that she only had twelve minutes, she couldn't spare any time to deal with her coworker's foolishness.

"I know you heard me, girl." Ever persistent, Casey Dunning sidled into Nona's office, a smirk on her face. "Did you get that thing I sent you?"

"Nah. Haven't checked my email today." Nona kept her eyes on her screen and her hands flying across the keys as she answered.

"Girl. You're such a workaholic. You're not even going to look at me?"

"Not until I hit Send on this article."

Casey sighed. "Fine. I'll wait."

For the next few moments, the only sound in the office was of Nona's seventy-five-words-per-minute typing. True to her word, she didn't acknowledge Casey until she'd completed the last line, run a quick spell-check and sent the article on its way. Raising her eyes to her perturbed-looking coworker, she asked, "What's so important?"

"It's not important, per se. But it is funny, and I think most of us in this office would agree that you're entirely too serious."

Nona rolled her eyes. "Forgive me, but I was under the impression that this was a newspaper office and not the writers' pen at a sketch comedy show."

Casey shook her head. "Ugh. Just check your email when you get a chance, okay? You're such a buzzkill."

Nona watched Casey as she strode out of the office, leaving the door open. "And yet you continue to try to change me."

After Casey left, Nona settled back in her chair. It was the end of another long day spent covering the Queen City's arts and entertainment scene for the *Charlotte Observer*. As department head, Nona enjoyed a good amount of editorial freedom in choosing the stories she chased—most of the time. But with that freedom came some heavy responsibilities. She was charged with leadership of the three other reporters who also covered the area, and with being the final set of eyes to see their articles before they were passed up to her boss, the editorial director.

The sound of someone else entering her office pulled Nona back to reality. She straightened in her chair as her boss, Wendell Huffman, strode into the space. "I just saw your article on the art gallery opening hit my inbox. Good work, ace."

She offered a small smile. "Thanks, Huff." It was what everyone in the office called him. At least everyone who'd been working at the paper more than a year.

At fifty-two, Wendell had been in the reporting game for more than two decades. His face was clean shaven and retained a youthful appearance despite the gray peppering the edges of his close-trimmed black hair. He had assessing brown eyes that seemed to see through a person and a laid-back personality that kept him calm even around the tightest of deadlines. Beneath his cool exterior, though, was a true passion for getting down to the real core of a story. Today he wore his regular uniform of a vertical-striped white shirt and a pair of crisply ironed khaki pants.

"Even though I haven't read it yet, I know it'll be gold." Wendell made himself comfortable in the chair on the other side of Nona's desk. "And that's why I have an assignment for you."

Nona's brow lifted in surprise and curiosity. "Really?" She chose most of her assignments, but when Wendell chose on her behalf, it usually meant the story would be a particularly compelling one.

"Yes. Are you familiar with the Grand Pearl Theater?"

She nodded. "The old building near J. C. Smith, on Beatties Ford Road, in Biddleville, right? It used to be the only black theater in town during segregation."

"Right. Well, the city has just shelled out millions to have it remodeled and restored, and get this…the architect is Asian, and a small business outfit at that. It's the biggest contract ever awarded by the city to a sole proprietor."

Nona's eyes widened. "Wow. A multimillion-dollar contract on a project like this, and it's not going to some global architecture conglomerate? *This* is news."

Wendell nodded. "You're telling me. The higher-ups at corporate are already buzzing about this, and the editor in chief called me about an hour ago. We want you to cover this."

Nona clapped her hands together as the excitement buzzed through her veins. "Sounds great! What's our angle? Are we looking at the rich history of the Grand Pearl and the surrounding neighborhood? Or are we attacking gentrification and lauding the city for its efforts at restoring an important landmark?"

"Actually, we're doing both of those angles. And a third angle."

"What's my third angle, Huff?"

"Learning everything there is to know about the architect, Ken Yamada. We want to know who he is, where he comes from, what he does in his spare time. But most of all, we want to know what drives him, what inspires his art. I'm told his winning design for the restoration is quite stunning."

Cupping her chin in her hand, Nona thought about

what Wendell was saying. It had been years since she'd
done a personal profile, but it hadn't been so long that
she'd forgotten how odd artists could be. "So I'm getting all up in this guy's business?"

"Basically." Wendell clasped his hands in front of
him, lacing his fingers. "There has to be something
remarkable about him. He beat out some pretty stiff
competition to get this contract."

"I agree." She knew that such an unprecedented contract could only have gone to someone like Mr. Yamada
because he had something that amazed and impressed
the city officials overseeing the project. "I'm on it."

Huff let a broad grin spread over his face. "Excellent. You'll start bright and early Monday morning on
this. There's a big unveiling of the new theater design
in three weeks, and we want to debut the feature a few
days before that."

Her jaw dropped. "A feature? As in front page of the
entertainment section?"

He rose from his chair. "No. As in, front page of the
paper, above the fold."

Holy crap. "I'm writing a headline feature?"

By now he was standing in her office doorway. "Yes,
if you can handle it. Can you get me a great story in
two and a half weeks?"

Parts of her were a tiny bit uncertain, but this was
the opportunity of a lifetime. It could make or break her
journalism career, and she decided she'd rather give it a
shot and risk screwing up than let the opportunity pass
by. "You got it, Huff. I'll get the story."

"That's what I like to hear, ace. Have a good weekend." With a tip of his imaginary hat, Wendell disappeared into the crowd of newspaper staffers headed home for the evening.

A glance at the clock showed Nona that it was already six thirty. She usually liked to be long gone from the office by this time, especially on a Friday. But as she sat at her desk turning Wendell's words over in her mind, she found it hard to focus on anything else. She sat there for several more minutes, jotting notes on a pad. Finally, as the janitor wheeled his cart into the main area of the newspaper office, Nona shut down her computer, gathered her belongings and left.

With a large cup of his favorite coffee in hand, Ken Yamada sat at the drafting table in his office. It was a beautiful summer morning in early June, and the weather was so nice it made Monday more tolerable. Spread out before him on the slanted surface of the table were the original floor plans for the Grand Pearl Theater, along with some historic photos of the structure. It had taken quite a bit of digging on the part of his assistant, Lynn, but they'd managed to obtain the floor plans along with images of the interior and exterior of the building. Seeing the theater in all its former glory brought a smile to Ken's face. He couldn't wait to get into the project and restore the Grand Pearl to greatness again.

Lynn entered then. A petite brunette in her late twenties, she wore dark slacks and a bright red cap-sleeve blouse. "So, do you think I've dug up enough information on the theater?" she asked before bringing her mug filled with the herbal tea she preferred to her lips.

Without looking back up from the bounty of images spread out before him, Ken nodded. "Yes, this should be sufficient. Thank you, Lynn."

"You're welcome." A twinkle of humor lit her blue eyes. "And I'm glad you said that, because I don't think I could've gotten you much more." She pulled up a stool next to Ken's and sat down.

As she came into his space, Ken could smell the aromatic scents of mint, citrus and bergamot rising from Lynn's steaming cup. He inhaled, enjoying the scents. He'd tried the tea once, after much prodding from Lynn. But he preferred to be caffeinated in the morning and wasn't a fan of the taste.

"Now that the city's on board and has accepted our proposal, we'll have to move quickly on this project." Ken jotted notes on a blank sticky paper with the charcoal pencil he kept tucked behind his ear most days. Affixing the small piece of paper to a corner of the drafting table, he added, "They've given us a tight turn-around on this. They expect to break ground the first week of July."

Lynn pursed her lips. "Wow. That is tight. So how closely are they expecting us to stick to the preliminary design plan you included with your proposal?"

He shrugged. "The committee says they like my vision, but they didn't really say I'd have to leave the plans unchanged."

She let her eyes roll up toward the ceiling. "You know me. I'm an 'if it ain't broke, don't fix it' kind of girl. It was your preliminary design that won the contract, so I think you should stick pretty close to it."

"That's true."

"However, I also like my job. So since you're the boss, I'm going to defer to you no matter what you decide." She winked, taking another sip from her mug of tea.

He chuckled. "Wise decision. Anyway, I'm thinking I will stick pretty closely to the preliminary design. My goal with the Grand Pearl Theater is twofold—I want to modernize the structure and pay homage to its rich history."

Lynn nodded. "I agree totally. I mean, look at these photos." She picked up one of the black-and-white images, which depicted three well-dressed African American couples standing in the theater's foyer. The caption read, *A Show at the Grand Pearl, 1956*. "I mean, it really was a grand place. The history surrounding it isn't the most pleasant, but it deserves to be honored."

"You're right. And upholding and honoring that history will play a large role in this project." Ken looked at the image of the smiling men and women, knowing the image was taken during a lighthearted moment. Still, as a man of color, he knew that life in America was much more complex for minorities. His own ancestors had been interned in a camp during the World War II era, and every day he encountered those who wished to define him only by tired old stereotypes of what an Asian man should be. He knew the specific issues were different for African Americans, but he couldn't help seeing the similarities in the way prejudice could affect the lives of people of color.

"So, what's first on the agenda, Ken?" Draining the last of her tea, Lynn set her mug aside on the edge of Ken's desk and waited for instructions.

Ken scratched his chin, his eyes sweeping over the image in front of him. "I want to start with the exterior building material and framework. Get in contact with a few stonemasonry companies and take their bids. I want to keep the exterior look very close to the original. After you've taken their bids, compile the data for me and we'll decide who to use for the project."

"I'm on it." Lynn slid from her stool and gathered her mug.

The ringing of Ken's desk phone broke the quiet in the room. Lynn leaned over the desk and picked up the handset. "Yamada Creative. This is Lynn. How may I assist you?"

Ken continued to make notes at the drafting table as his assistant listened to whoever was on the other end.

"Okay. Hold, please." Lynn cupped her hand over the mouthpiece. "It's a reporter from the *Charlotte Observer*. She wants to speak with you about the Grand Pearl project."

And so it begins. Ken knew that news of his contract would spread quickly, due to the dollar amount he'd been paid. While he wasn't a fan of reporters, he understood the interest. Reaching out for the handset, he said, "I'll take it." No use putting off the inevitable.

Lynn passed Ken the phone.

"Hello? This is Ken Yamada."

"Mr. Yamada, good morning."

"Good morning." He cradled the phone between his head and his shoulder and listened to the female reporter list her name and credentials. A few seconds passed before he noticed that Lynn was still standing by his desk, watching him, as if her feet were glued to the spot.

He frowned, waving his hand and mouthing, "Get out."

Lynn snickered, but did as she was told. After she'd left the room, he turned his attention back to the woman on the phone, who was still going on about the feature she planned to write.

"Miss, that sounds great. However I'm on a tight deadline, so could we please get to the purpose of your call?"

She stopped chattering, and her tone held a bit of censure as she asked, "When and where could you meet me for an initial interview, Mr. Yamada?"

He felt his brow crease into a frown. "Initial? How many interviews do you think this is going to take?"

"I'm not sure, but I'll take up as little of your time as I possibly can."

His frown deepened. He was a private man, and he didn't enjoy having his time or his personal space infringed upon, least of all by a stranger. "We can meet tomorrow morning, 9:00 a.m., at the Starbucks in Charlotte Plaza. Are you familiar with it?"

"Very. I'll see you there. And thank you, Mr. Yamada."

He rose from the stool to replace the phone in the

cradle. And as he stood in the quiet of his office, he wondered what he'd gotten himself into.

He'd have to be careful with this reporter. She seemed like the eager type who'd ask him probing questions and try to uncover his entire life story for her own purposes.

But no matter what she had planned, he couldn't let her do that.

Because there were parts of his life that no one could ever know about.

Chapter 2

With a cup of iced coffee and a warm croissant in hand, Nona slid into a seat at a table for two near the front of Starbucks Tuesday morning. It was eight thirty, well before the time she was scheduled to meet with Ken Yamada, but she'd come in early for several reasons. First, she needed to get something in her stomach and get caffeinated so she could be fully ready for this crucial first interview.

The other reason she'd come in early was to snag the right table. It needed to be small so that she would be sitting in close proximity to her interview subject. She found that nearness made people more likely to open up. The table also needed to be near the front so she could see him when he walked in. After years of doing in-person interviews, she'd become an expert at reading people: their stride, their expression and their body language.

She munched on her croissant, washing it down with a sip of the cold, sweetened coffee. While she ate, she wondered what Ken would be like in person. Their brief phone interaction had given her very little to go on. From that conversation, she could only tell that he had a deep voice, that he was a busy person and that he wasn't a fan of being interviewed. He'd been pleasant with her but still managed to be a bit brusque when he'd asked her how many interviews she'd need.

She settled into her seat, pulling out her phone. She'd made sure it was fully charged so she could use its recording app to capture their conversation. Beyond that, she'd brought along her charger, just in case. She considered being prepared to be one of her greatest strengths.

She was scrolling through her email when the phone rang and her best friend's face and name appeared on the caller ID. Knowing she still had at least ten minutes until Ken would arrive, she swiped to answer the call. "Hey, girl."

"Hey, Nona." Hadley Monroe, Nona's closest pal since college, sounded chipper as ever. "What's up in the big city?"

Nona chuckled at Hadley's quip. "I'm guessing most places are big cities when you compare them to Sapphire Shores."

Hadley popped her lips, the familiar sound reverberating in Nona's ear. "Nona, don't be hating on my little slice of paradise. But for real, what are you up to today? Anything interesting?"

"I'm actually at a coffee shop, waiting for an interview subject to arrive. Remember the feature I told you about Saturday?"

It sounded like she was chewing something. Between bites, Hadley spoke. "Yeah. The one about the architect and the old opera house or something."

Nona rolled her eyes. "It's a theater. But yes, I'm interviewing the architect today."

Hadley stopped chewing. "Oh, girl. Is he fine? Have you seen him?"

"No, he hasn't gotten here yet, so I don't know what he looks like."

"Um, hello, Ms. Ace Reporter. We have this invention now where you can look people up. Have you heard of it? It's called the internets." Her tone was rich in sarcastic humor.

"Shut up, Hadley. You know I have a very specific method of doing my stories. I never web search someone until I've met them in person. I don't want anything clouding my first impression of them." That had always been her policy, and it had never failed her, so she didn't plan on changing it any time soon. Balancing the phone on her shoulder, she spread her favorite pens in front of her. She rarely took handwritten notes due to advances in technology, but she liked to have the pens there anyway.

"All right, whatever. But I'm expecting a call after you meet him. If he's fine, I wanna know about it." The sounds on Hadley's end of the line included the rattling of pots and pans and running water.

"Hadley, what are you doing? There's a lot of background noise."

"I just finished breakfast and now I'm washing up my dishes before I head over to the office."

"Another fun-filled day at Monroe Properties, eh?" Nona chuckled, knowing most people would be very happy with having an ocean view from their desk. But since Hadley worked for the family business and often complained about feeling stifled, she probably saw things differently.

Hadley sighed. "Yes, girl. But at least Savion is on vacation this week, so I only have to deal with Campbell. Working with family ain't easy."

"Let me get off the phone. I've got an interview and you've got to go do your brother's bidding. I'll talk to you later."

"'Bye, girl." Hadley disconnected the call.

As the phone returned to the home screen, Nona glanced at the time in the upper right corner. *Nine twenty? Where is this guy?* She hoped he had a damn good excuse for being late, because she considered punctuality very important. She placed the phone on the tabletop and let her gaze move to the doorway.

Just as she looked toward the door, it swung open, and in walked a dark-haired man she assumed to be Ken Yamada. He wore dark sunglasses, a button-down shirt in a soft shade of blue and navy blue slacks. A belt with a gold buckle depicting two crossed swords encircled his trim waist. He was taller than she'd expected, and his upper body was muscled but not beefy. He moved with a sure stride, his entire manner radiating a confidence that bordered on arrogance.

She stood at the table and called out to him at just above normal volume. "Mr. Yamada?"

His head swiveled her way. "That's me." And he turned, began moving in her direction.

She watched his approach, wondering when he would take off his sunglasses. She knew she could get a much better read on him if she could see his eyes.

When he entered her space, he stopped. Lifting his hand, he removed his sunglasses and tucked them into his shirt pocket, looking down as he did so.

"I'm Nona Gregory with the *Charlotte Observer*." She stuck out her hand.

When he looked back up at her, with his eyes in full view, Nona's heart skipped a beat. *Damn.* He had the most beautiful, expressive brown eyes she'd ever seen. They were rich and dark, only a shade lighter than the jet black of his hair. A few moments passed with her staring into his eyes, silent and entranced.

The corners of his mouth lifted in a slight smile as he gave her hand a brief shake, then released it. "It's nice to meet you. Are we going to sit?"

His words reached her ears, working their way to her brain for processing.

Snapping out of her trance, she gestured him toward his seat. "Yes. Thank you for meeting me, Mr. Yamada, although I wish you'd been on time."

The smile faded as quickly as it appeared. "I'm sorry, Headmistress. Are you going to give me detention?"

She cocked a brow. Apparently, the architect was no

pushover. "I'll let it slide this time, since it's your first infraction." She gestured to the table. "Shall we sit, or do you care to grab a coffee?"

"I'll get a drink first, if you don't mind." His tone was dry, and his expression told her that he had fully intended to get his drink, whether she minded or not.

"Go ahead." She sat back down and watched him walk away. As he stood at the counter ordering a beverage, she watched his every move. His steps were somewhat stiff now, a contrast to the way he'd moved when he'd walked in. His body language had changed as well. His shoulders were squared, hands clenched at his side. He looked more ready for a fistfight than an interview.

Then and there, Nona knew she would have her work cut out. He was guarded, and she was going to have to come up with some way to get him to reveal himself to her.

And she'd have to do it while trying to ignore how hot he was and how gorgeous his eyes were.

This wouldn't be an easy interview. But she'd never been one to back down from a challenge.

While he waited for his dark roast, Ken purposefully kept his eyes on the barista dispensing it. He didn't want to look back at Nona, because he sensed her watching him. She'd been assessing him from the moment he walked in. While he understood her scrutiny was likely rooted in journalistic curiosity, he still didn't like it. He was a private man, always had been. The last thing he needed was someone to stare him down in some vain attempt to discover his deepest personal secrets.

He shot a sidelong glance in her direction, making sure not to turn his head as he did. He could see her in the periphery of his field of vision. She was gorgeous, and he'd noticed that as soon as he'd seen her. She was tall, probably close to his height. Her skin was the color of rich earth, and her hair was dark brown with a few streaks of bronze. She wore a sleeveless white blouse and a pair of yellow slacks that hugged her hips before flaring into wide-leg pants.

The moment he'd seen her sitting at the table, her back as stiff as a board, with about seven pens lined up in front of her, he'd pegged her as uptight. When she'd shaken his hand, she'd only confirmed his suspicions. He decided to entertain himself throughout this initial meeting with her. She probably wouldn't like it, but that wasn't any of his concern.

After he sweetened the mug of steaming coffee to his liking, he rejoined her at the table. She was scrolling through something on her phone, but she immediately set it aside when he took his seat.

"Since we're getting a late start, I'd like to begin right away." She set her phone on the table and took care positioning it.

He leaned against the hard wooden backrest of his chair, his coffee in hand. As he tried to get comfortable, he realized the stiffness of the chair mimicked that of his interviewer. *How can a woman this beautiful be so uptight?* "Okay. Where do we begin?"

Her hazel eyes locked on him, she said, "First of all, I need to let you know that I'm recording our interview with an app on my smartphone. I find it helps me with

my article if I revisit the recordings later during my
writing process."

"I understand." He drank from his ceramic mug, letting the rich warmth of the coffee wash down his throat.

"Good. Then let's begin with the basics. Who is Ken
Yamada?"

He snorted. The sound came out before he could
stop it.

Her brow hitched, lips thinning as her expression
went sour. "Is there something amusing about my question, Mr. Yamada?"

"Call me Ken, please. No need to be so formal."

"Fine. What's so funny, Ken?" She watched him,
her brow furrowed as if she were honestly confused
by his amusement.

"It's a little cliché, don't you think? I mean, you're
opening our interview with some existential query?"
He took another drink of coffee.

She rolled her eyes, then took a breath. Her professional demeanor returned to replace the coolness that
had been rolling off her only seconds before. "Ken, I'm
sure you already know this, but the contract you just
won from the city is unprecedented in terms of scope
and money."

He set his mug down, rubbed his hands together.
"Yes, that's true." But what she didn't know was how
long and hard he'd worked to win the contract. *I deserve
that contract. Hell, I earned it.*

"I'm not trying to psychoanalyze you, Ken. I know
the people of Charlotte are curious about the phenom
behind the Grand Pearl project, and I simply want to

give them the most complete, accurate portrait of you that I can."

He sensed the truth in her words right away. It was obvious that Nona was a consummate journalist, determined to deliver her very best work to her readers. He supposed he could respect that, since as an artist, he wanted the same thing for every one of his projects. "I get it."

"I'm glad you understand. Now, what can you tell me about your early days? Tell me about your upbringing. Did you always know you wanted to be an architect?"

He bristled at the mention of his upbringing. "I don't really want to talk about my childhood."

"Is there any particular reason?"

He sensed her probing. "Yes. It isn't relevant. I didn't decide to pursue architecture until my second year in college."

She pursed her lips. "Okay. Let me ask you this. Are you any relation to Hiro Yamada, who was formerly Mecklenburg County commissioner?"

A slow nod was the only answer he gave.

She watched him closely. "I'm going to guess you don't want to elaborate on your relationship to Mr. Yamada?"

"No, and as I understood it, he was not the subject of the interview." He fought down the irritation that usually arose when he felt someone getting too close. He didn't mind answering her questions—as long as she stuck to the topic at hand.

"Maybe we'll revisit that at another time, then."

He folded his arms across his chest. "No, we won't."

She took a slow breath, tapped the tips of her French-manicured nails on the table. "You know, we aren't making much progress with this, Ken."

"Are you suggesting that's my fault?"

"You don't seem willing to share much about your life. In order to really nail this article, I have to get to know you on a deeper level."

He leaned forward in his chair, holding eye contact with her. "Look, I'll answer any questions you have that pertain to my *work*. That's what this is about, isn't it? About the Grand Pearl project and how I operate my business?"

She held his gaze, letting him know she wasn't intimidated. "Yes, that is the basis of the article. But there has to be information about who you are as a person, because that informs your art."

He could feel his jaw tighten. "I'm not interested in rehashing my entire past for the entertainment of the faceless populace."

This time she dropped her gaze and sighed. "Fine. But I'm telling you, the piece will read as shallow and empty if you insist on leaving out your past."

He shrugged. "I can't say I care. I already locked down the project, and I'm not trying to win a popularity contest."

She looked at him quizzically, blinked a few times, as if she didn't believe what she'd just heard him say. "That was a very arrogant statement."

"You say arrogant. I say confident."

She picked up her phone and began swiping the

screen. "I'm going to stop recording now. We obviously aren't going to get anywhere today."

"We could have, if you had adjusted your line of questioning."

Irritation flashed in her eyes. "I don't tell you how to design a building, so don't tell me how to go about my writing process."

He drained the rest of his coffee, watching her as she gathered her things.

"Congratulations. You just guaranteed that the interview process is going to take longer." She tucked her phone into her purse and stood from her seat.

"I'll wait to hear from you, then."

Standing next to the table, with a frown marring her beautiful face, she asked, "Will you actually answer my questions the next time? I don't like having my time wasted."

"Neither do I. So yes, I will."

"I'll be in touch." Slinging the strap of her purse over her shoulder, she turned and walked away.

As he watched her retreat, Ken smiled to himself. Even in the throes of annoyance, Nona was still beautiful and sexy as hell. He knew she probably thought he was an arrogant jerk, but in reality, he was just protecting his past. In order to keep the people he loved safe, he didn't have any other choice.

Watching her hips sway as she strode out of the coffee shop brightened his smile.

He couldn't wait to see what their next encounter would bring.

Chapter 3

Stifling a yawn, Nona dragged herself into the kitchen for a cup of tea. It was early enough that she'd beat the sun out of bed, and mornings like this, she seriously wondered why she'd pursued journalism.

She fiddled around in the dark for a few moments before locating the switch. Her bleary eyes protested as the room flooded with bright light. Padding to the cabinet, she took down her mug and went to get her tea bags.

On cue, Sheba trotted into the kitchen. The two-year-old black lab immediately came to where Nona stood and nuzzled her bare calf with her cool, wet nose.

As always, Sheba's presence brought a smile to Nona's face. "Good morning, girl." Leaving her tea supplies on the counter, she squatted down to give her sweet pup a few snuggles. Back on her feet, she washed

her hands and started the teakettle. Then she fixed
Sheba bowls of fresh kibble and water before grabbing
her own breakfast ingredients from the white French-
door refrigerator.

Twenty minutes later, she sat at the small table by
her kitchen window. With her hot tea, a banana and an
egg and cheese on an English muffin, she watched the
sun rise. Sheba, having finished her kibble, lay quietly
at Nona's feet beneath the table.

As she sipped from her mug, she thought back on the
previous day's disastrous interview with Ken Yamada.
She could clearly recall her feelings the moment she'd
first seen him: a mixture of irritation and attraction. She
hadn't been pleased with his tardiness, but she'd definitely been pleased with his looks. He was handsome
in a way that couldn't be ignored. He was well dressed,
confident and had a killer smile. Not to mention he had
a head full of raven-black hair and dark, mesmerizing
eyes. She could easily have stared at him all day and
never gotten tired of the view.

Ken was unlike any other man she'd ever encountered, and that had turned out to be both good and bad.
While she loved the way he looked and the subtle yet
undeniable masculinity he exuded, she couldn't figure
out why he'd been so reluctant to share his past with
her. The man was about as secretive as a government
spy. She'd gone there hoping to learn something about
who he was as a person, but he'd given her nothing.
She'd never had an interview subject shut down on her
that way.

What Ken didn't know was that his insistence on

being evasive only fueled her curiosity. Their encounter had made her more determined than ever to find out what made him tick. It also made her think he had something to hide, something he didn't want the public to know. Who or what was he protecting? Before their association ended, Nona was determined to discover the answers.

Finishing up her breakfast, Nona straightened up and went to get dressed. She was grateful that she didn't have to be in to the newspaper office until ten today. She'd still gotten up at her usual time because she planned to consult the internet to do a bit of digging. She wanted to see what she could find out about Ken's life before she took Sheba out for a morning run.

Once she'd dressed in her running shorts, tank and sneakers, she eased onto her couch with her laptop. Sheba took up residence on the empty cushion next to her with her furry face pressed against Nona's thigh.

Opening a browser window, Nona performed a basic search on Ken. That search pulled up very little, but the top two results were somewhat helpful. One was an inactive profile from one of those classmate connection websites, which listed Ken as a graduate of Independence High School. The other was an article on running in Charlotte from a fitness magazine. There was a photo of Ken along with a quote about how much he enjoyed running at Freedom Park. Nona made a mental note of those tidbits as well as the name and email of the writer of the article. Obviously that person had had some success with interviewing Ken and had even managed to get a photo out of him.

In a separate window, she shot off a quick email to
the writer, hoping to garner some tips on how to get
Ken to open up. The running article was fairly recent,
having been published in the past six months. That gave
her hope that the writer would remember her interac-
tions with Ken and be able to offer some insight. At this
point, Nona would take whatever help she could get.

Next she performed a search of Ken's name in con-
junction with Hiro Yamada. The way Ken had bristled
at the mention of Hiro's name let her know there was
definitely a close association between them. Hiro had
served as county commissioner during the late '70s
and early '80s, so she checked the image search results
to see what the former official had looked like during
his tenure. When she placed the image of Hiro in the
'70s next to the photo of Ken from the fitness magazine, the resemblance immediately became apparent.
Nona smiled.

*I'd bet my press pass that Hiro and Ken are father
and son.* There wasn't any other logical conclusion. Ken
was basically the identical twin of a young Hiro. That
would also explain why Ken had become so agitated
when she brought up Hiro's name. Ken had been particularly unwilling to talk about his upbringing. What
better way to get to the root of someone's childhood
experiences than to bring up their parent?

Going a bit deeper into the image results, she came
across a family portrait. It had been taken for the *Observer* as part of a profile on Hiro during the time he
occupied the commissioner's seat. It showed a young

Hiro with his arms around a demurely dressed young woman, who in turn cradled a baby.

The caption read: *Commissioner Yamada with his wife and son.* Nona knew the baby was probably Ken. But while her dash through the internet had revealed a few things to her, it also left her with so many more questions. Why had Ken tried to hide the fact that Hiro was his father? And why had he been so reluctant to talk about his childhood? The family photo seemed to show two loving parents doting over their precious infant. But she'd been around long enough to know that looks could be deceiving.

Sheba began whimpering from her spot on the couch, a telltale sign of the pup's restlessness. She nudged Nona's thigh, further communicating her need to go outside.

"All right. Let's go run, girl." She shut down the computer, slid it into a blue laptop sleeve and set it on the coffee table. Grabbing the leash, her house keys and her phone, she tucked them into the fanny pack she wore when she ran.

Just as she started to zip the pack, her phone buzzed. Checking it, she saw that the writer from the fitness magazine had replied to her message. Thankful that the reporter had gotten back to her so quickly, she clicked the leash buckle to Sheba's collar, then opened the email.

Good morning.
Just saw your message. Yes, I remember Mr. Yamada. He's a hard nut to crack. The best way to get

him to talk is to run with him. That's what I had to do. It seems to relax him and gets him to open up. You mentioned he's very evasive, and he was initially the same way with me. Even if you're not a runner, if you don't get out on the trail with him, expect more of the same. Best of luck,
M. Hargrove

Smiling, Nona tucked the phone away. Now she had what she needed to get Ken to tell his story. Luckily, she happened to be a frequent runner and was in very good shape. Since she and Ken were close in height, she was sure she could keep up with him on the trail.

As she headed out the door with Sheba, she started planning how to make this run with Ken happen.

The interior of the kendo room at Satori Martial Arts was filled with the sounds of shouting, feet stamping and wood striking wood. The noises echoed in Ken's ears, partly because he was making some of them as he and Marco moved around the wooden floor, sparring. Their bare feet made a shushing sound as they slid over the floor's surface, then a boom as they stomped in time with the thrusts of their bamboo swords.

Their bodies were encased in traditional practice clothes. The outfit worn frequently by students and those who sparred casually consisted of loose-fitting white jackets and trousers. Because they were friends and didn't spar for competition, they generally didn't wear the full kendo armor.

When the match ended, and both men bowed to each

other, Marco groaned. "You know, I'm tired of coming here to spar with you and getting beat every time."

Ken shrugged as the two of them left the sparring floor. "I told you to practice more often. How do you expect to improve without practice?"

They entered the locker room, where Marco shrugged out of his sweaty shirt. "I don't have time. And now that I'm married, I have even less time."

With a shake of his head, Ken stuffed his own damp clothes into his gym bag. "It's about commitment. You're not committed."

"You should *be* committed. My loyalty is to Joi." Marco pulled a towel and his shower caddy from his locker and started moving toward the showers. "It's strange that everything that excites you involves wooden sticks. You work with a pencil, play drums for the band and then come here and swing a bamboo sword for kicks."

"What can I say? I'm a steady guy." Ken chuckled and punched Marco in the shoulder as he walked by.

After the men had showered and changed, they moved to the snack bar. Seated at a small table with two protein shakes, they continued their conversation.

"Are you ever going to get serious about kendo?"

"No." Marco didn't hesitate with his answer. "To be honest, I don't know how I let you talk me into coming here in the first place. We both know I'm a lover, not a fighter."

Ken laughed. "Based on how much you suck at this, I'd have to agree."

Taking a drink of his shake, Marco frowned. "You

know what? I'm not coming back here. When I was single and had free time to kill, that was one thing. But now that I'm married, I see no reason to leave my beautiful wife just to come here and be insulted by the likes of you."

Ken shook his head. "Do you even know what kendo means? What it's all about?"

"I don't, but I'm sure you'll enlighten me."

"Yeah, I will. Kendo means 'the way of the sword.' It has its basis in the time-honored tradition of Japanese swordsmanship. It builds character, increases physical strength and…"

"Blah, blah, blah." Marco rolled his eyes. "You know what else builds my character and increases my physical strength? Being home with my wife."

Ken could see he was losing this battle. "I get it, Marco. I won't be upset if you decide not to come back to the dojo."

"Good, because I'm not," he said as he finished up his smoothie. "What's going on with you and the newspaper reporter, by the way? Told her your life story yet?"

"Actually I haven't told her much of anything." He leaned back in his chair, remembering how irritated Nona had looked when she'd left the coffee shop that day. "Trust me, it wasn't due to lack of effort on her part."

"What do you mean?"

"I understand that she's trying to collect information and that it's part of her job. But she comes across as a little…pushy."

Marco shrugged. "What did you expect? Like you said, she has a job to do. Why do you insist on making it hard for her?"

Ken looked past Marco, through the window. Outside, the sun was setting, and the city lights that illuminated the streets of the Queen City by night were starting to appear. He thought of his past and his present. Even though he considered Marco his closest friend, there were many things about Ken's life that Marco didn't know. "I have my reasons."

Groaning, Marco got up from his seat. "If you say so. At any rate, she seems like the type who isn't going to give up. If you want to get her out of your hair, you're going to have to answer some questions."

As vexing as it was, Ken knew Marco was right. Nona Gregory did not strike him as a woman who'd be content with failure. She didn't even seem like the type who'd be satisfied with knowing him on the surface level, either. No, she was going to keep digging and digging until she hit pay dirt.

That dogged determination to know everything about him was what worried him the most.

"Listen. I need to get home to Joi. She's making my favorite dessert tonight."

"What's that?"

"Whipped cream."

"What?" He couldn't make any sense of his friend's answer.

Marco winked. "Strategically placed whipped cream. Get yourself a good woman and you too can enjoy this decadent treat."

Shaking his head, Ken grabbed their empty cups. "Get out of here, Marco."

"With pleasure."

Ken tossed the cups in the trash as Marco made his way out the door.

Chapter 4

As dawn painted the sky on Thursday morning, Nona stood by a bench in Freedom Park. Dressed in her close-fitting running pants and a black tee, she stretched by lifting first one ankle, then the other, behind her bottom. Sheba sat dutifully at Nona's feet with her leash looped around the bench armrest. The dog's steady breathing was the only sound that competed with the chirping of birds and the soft morning breeze rustling the grass and trees.

The bench Nona had staked out was strategically located near the only entry point to the park's running trail. As she stood, bouncing in place to prime her muscles for the upcoming run, she smiled.

He'll be here any minute.

She'd spoken with Ken briefly by phone Wednesday

evening and had asked if she could accompany him on his morning run in order to chat with him. To her surprise, he'd agreed right away. Now all that was left was to keep up with him, but she didn't have any worries about that. She was in incredible shape due to her own running and other fitness habits.

The sound of an engine pulled her attention toward the nearby parking lot. The two-door coupe slipped into a spot a few places down from her car, and the driver cut the engine.

When Ken stepped out of the car, Nona's gaze fixed on him.

He looked somewhat different in the early morning light, dressed in his running clothes. He wore a sleeveless white shirt and a pair of dark blue running shorts, which left the muscled expanse of his arms and legs visible. As he walked her way, the muscles flexed in time with his movements.

Her heart began to pound in her ears. When she'd met him a few days ago in his business casual dress, she would never have imagined he was built so solidly. She swallowed to empty her mouth, which suddenly watered. Reaching to her waist, she pulled the water bottle from her pack and took a quick swig.

Entering her space with an easy smile, he spoke. "Good morning."

"Morning," she managed.

He stooped down to give Sheba's head a rub. "Cute pup. You two ready?"

She smiled. Sheba hadn't backed away from him

to indicate any dislike. That was a good sign. "Yes, we're ready."

They walked to the trail ahead as Nona held the end of Sheba's leash.

"I see you're on time today," Nona teased.

"I'm never late for my runs." Ken squatted to tie his shoelace, moving fluidly into the runner's mark stance. "I suppose you have more questions about my life?"

She shrugged. "Of course I do. You didn't give me anything last time."

"You knew I run here."

"I found that out on my own."

He chuckled. "Beat me back to the trailhead, and we'll talk."

Her face scrunched into a frown. "You didn't say that on the phone."

"Those are my terms." He raised his hips, indicating his impending start.

Matching him, Nona drew a deep breath.

He took off like a shot, his powerful legs propelling him forward.

She followed a second later and soon matched his pace.

Sheba kept up with both of them, allowing her youthful energy to have its head.

While Nona ran, cutting through the humid morning air like a knife, she thought about his trickery. In his overconfidence, he obviously thought he'd beat her in this impromptu footrace and then be released from any obligation to speak to her. She had no intention of letting him off the hook, so she made sure to keep her strides long.

When he glanced to his left and saw her easily keeping pace with him, a flicker of worry crossed his face. It was only there for a moment before he kicked into second gear and picked up his pace.

With a smile, Nona sped up as well. The wind whipped her ponytail as Sheba ran alongside her. She felt powerful, exhilarated. There was nothing like a morning run to get the blood pumping and the gears turning.

Sheba reached the trailhead first, followed closely by her mistress.

When Ken got there, he leaned over, placing his large hands on his knees as he caught his breath.

Nona, still standing upright, felt winded yet triumphant. "What's the matter? Didn't get your coffee this morning?"

He stood, making a show of rolling his eyes at her. "Oh, please. The dog obviously tugged you across the finish line."

Sheba cocked her head to the side, as if she took offense.

Nona waved her hand dismissively. "Whatever. Don't be a sore loser." She pointed to the bench. "Now, you owe me an interview, sir."

As if admitting defeat, he trudged over to the bench and plopped down. "Three questions. Ask away."

Parts of her wanted to kick him in the shin. "After all that, all I get is three questions?"

He nodded. "For now, yes."

She shook her head. He certainly had an odd way of approaching things. Having interviewed artists in the past, this wasn't her first time encountering this type of behavior. "Fine."

He watched her as she called Sheba to sit and joined him on the bench. "What do you want to know?"

"Plenty, but we'll start with this." She laid her smartphone on her lap and set it to record. "Mr. Yamada, when did you first sense that you wanted to pursue the arts?"

He raised a hand to scratch his chin, his gaze fixed on some faraway point. "I was in college, majoring in computer graphics. We completed a class project that involved developing plans and schematics for a fictional skyscraper. I'd always loved to draw for as long as I could remember. But when we worked on that project, I fell in love with architecture. It's the meeting of math, science and art."

She nodded, both impressed and intrigued by his answer. "I see. My next question is, what was the first architectural design of your professional career?"

"Hmm. When I first opened Yamada Creative a few years back, I took on a project to build a new library for Duck, North Carolina. It's a very small town, and their entire collection fit into a one-story building of about seventy-five hundred square feet. It wasn't a glamorous project, but I was able to provide the residents of Duck with a new facility that met their needs."

She was enjoying discovering some facts about Ken's architecture work. If she were honest with herself, she'd admit that she was also enjoying his company. Aware that she only had one question left, she decided to make it a good one. "What has been your favorite project so far?"

He didn't hesitate. "The children's hospital in Lillyville. My team and I worked on the design over the course of eight or nine months. The town didn't have a proper facility for kids with serious injuries and diseases, and we took that into consideration in our design. We wanted to build something that incorporated meeting the medical needs of very sick children while also conveying a sense of whimsy and playfulness. I think we accomplished that."

"Wow. You speak very passionately about the hospital project."

He smiled, turning her way. "It's definitely the one I'm most proud of. I still go over there about once a month to visit with the patients and just enjoy what I created."

Her eyes connected with his, and a prickle ran up her spine. Hearing the way he spoke about the children's hospital touched her in a way she hadn't expected.

His voice broke into her thoughts. "That was your last question."

"I know." She continued to keep eye contact with him, not wanting the moment to end.

He leaned closer, the heat of his body radiating out to mingle with hers. "Are you saying you're satisfied?"

She didn't move away. "Not at all. I'd love to see your office."

"Why?"

"Seeing your workspace may help me understand

you better. I may not even need to ask you much else."
She inhaled, taking in the scent of his woodsy deodorant.

"I'm okay with that. Call me and we'll set it up."

Before she could draw her next breath, he placed a peck on her cheek.

"What...?" she stammered. She'd been caught off guard, but she couldn't say she hadn't enjoyed it. The warmth spreading from her cheek made her reach up to place her hand there.

He smiled, his dark eyes twinkling.

She got the distinct sense that he enjoyed seeing her so off-kilter.

"Have a good day, Nona."

Without another word, he strode to his car, got in and drove away.

Nona sat on the bench for several minutes, gathering her focus.

Saturday morning, Ken gathered with the rest of the Queen City Gents at Marco's house for band rehearsal. As the four of them set up their instruments in Marco's spare room, Ken looked around at the faces of the men he considered to be his closest friends. Each man wore a smile, one that seemed to have been put there by the woman in his life. Shaking his head, Ken eased onto the stool behind his drum set, and began tapping out a simple rhythm on the snare and kick tom to warm up.

Soon, Ken segued into "Drum Waltz," which he'd learned from the techniques of his idol, jazz drum great Max Roach. The cadence moved in three-quarter time, making use of almost the entire drum set. As Roach had done, Ken threw in taps on the rims and outer casings of the drums to increase the depth and variety of sounds he could make.

As was usually the case when the guys sensed Ken was in the zone, conversation in the room ceased as Ken ran through the waltz a couple of times then moved into a freestyle, improvised rhythm. He was used to having inspiration grab hold of him this way, but the source of today's inspiration was a surprise. In his mind's eye, he pictured Nona in her fitted running gear. She had a body built for pleasure, and he would have to have been blind not to see that. As he remembered her tall, lithe figure, his drumming slowed but became richer, more passionate. Before he knew it, he'd slipped into a sensual, lilting ride cadence. His sticks struck the cymbals and the snare in a pattern reminiscent of the movements of her body as he imagined her slowly strutting toward him. His lips stretched into a smile.

Nona Gregory is a whole lot of woman.

When Ken finally looked up from his drum set, he saw Darius, Marco and Rashad all staring at him. No one said a word.

Ken's brow crinkled. "What?"

Still, no one responded.

Ken chuckled, shaking his head. "You act like you never saw me get into a groove before. Darius, pick your jaw up off the floor. And Rashad, you look like your eyes are about to pop out of your head. Fix your face, man!"

Marco spoke first as the other two men tried to

straighten up. "Sure, we've seen you in a groove before. We've all been there. But this is different."

Ken shrugged. "I don't know what you mean."

Taking a few steps closer to Ken, Darius looked closely at him. "It's a woman."

Ken frowned.

"Oh, it's definitely a woman." Rashad clapped his hands together. "Wow. I never thought I'd see the day."

Marco added, "I know who it is. It's the reporter from the newspaper, right? The one who's writing the story about you?"

"And what makes you think I have any interest in her?" Ken set his sticks on the snare, folding his arms over his chest.

"You spent almost an hour complaining about her when we sparred in kendo this week." Marco folded his arms over his chest, mirroring Ken.

"You've never cared enough about a woman to mention her name to any one of us, let alone talk about her for that long." Darius shook his head, eyes wide with amazement. "I think it's finally happening."

Ken groaned. He never would have thought someone could make him regret his fantasy. If he'd known his thoughts were so plainly displayed on his face, he'd have tucked his daydream away until he was alone.

"I'm glad a woman has finally gotten under your skin. I was beginning to worry about you, bro." Rashad took a seat behind the keyboard he used for rehearsals.

"Looks like our last single member is about to be taken down, boys." Darius chuckled as he set his upright bass, Miss Molly, on its stand.

"Whatever. You guys are full of crap." Ken waved them off, already sensing the futility of the discussion. His bandmates were always bringing up his singlehood; it had been that way ever since Marco had married Joi a couple of months ago. Now that they knew he'd been thinking about a woman, there was no way they'd quit harping on it.

"I just want to know her name." The remark came from Darius.

When Ken didn't answer, Marco volunteered the information. "Her name is Nona."

"I'd love to meet her." Rashad played his hands over the keys. "Just to say thanks for taking Ken down a peg."

Rolling his eyes, Ken vowed not to mention that he'd kissed Nona. He saw no need to add fuel to this fire. "Can we just get on with rehearsal?"

Darius grinned. "As much as I like teasing Ken, he's right. We really should get to work on this week's set."

Conversation turned toward the music the band would play and away from Ken's personal life. Relieved, he grabbed his sticks and waited for Rashad's cue.

In the back of his mind, he thought of Nona and the problem she presented. He'd agreed to let her interview him for the newspaper because no sensible businessman would turn down good publicity. But being attracted to Nona had come as a surprise, something he'd never considered would be part of the equation. The way she made him feel only served to further complicate an already complex situation. He was a private man, and letting someone into his personal life was difficult enough without the added burden of growing attraction.

He knew he'd have to work doubly hard now. He had to protect his single status as well as his privacy, no matter how intoxicating the determined reporter might be.

Chapter 5

"Okay, ladies and gentlemen. I need your attention on me, please."

Nona stood before her intermediate jazz dance class, dressed in her leggings, tank and felt-bottom dancing shoes. Her students, ranging in age from eleven to fourteen, were lined up in front of her. All ten of her students were present, eight girls and two boys, each standing on their designated mark on the wooden floor.

She'd been teaching this class two nights a week at Butterfly Ballet and Dance for the past five years, and she truly loved the work. It wasn't the highest-paying gig in the world, but the joy she got from working with her students and seeing them improve their art more than made up for the paltry paycheck. Her parents' prodding, and the sense of obligation she felt to them, had led her into journalism as a main career. Pure passion drove her to teach dance.

As the children settled down, ending their conversations and focusing on her, she smiled. "Thank you. Today, we'll continue to work on our turns as a basis for our recital choreography. Everybody into first position parallel, please." She moved into the position, standing with her feet eight inches apart and her toes pointed forward.

The children mimicked her stance.

"Second position legs." She waited as the children adjusted. "Now add second position arms."

Over the next forty minutes, Nona walked her students through the practice of a series of turn maneuvers. Moving between the two rows of students, she stopped to reposition little arms and feet as they executed paddle turns, piques and pirouettes. They worked hard, staying focused even as they repeated the same maneuver over and over again. When they achieved good form and proper execution, Nona heaped them with praise for their efforts.

The intermediate group was full of students who'd begun dance lessons as young children, some as young as four or five years old. Those who didn't like dance or didn't feel capable enough to handle it usually dropped out before the intermediate level. By the time they reached Nona's class, they were serious about learning all they could. Their interest level and dedication were growing, with many of them eager to move on to advanced classes. They were still excited about dancing but knew they had a lot more to learn, and that was what appealed to her about teaching students at that level.

As the end of class approached, Nona had her students sit on the floor in a circle, as usual. Sitting down between two of the kids, she looked around at their faces. "Great class today, everyone. Now, let's have our chat. Who has something they want to talk about today?"

Class chats were something Nona had implemented early in her dance teaching days. Due to the age of her students, they often were facing complex issues at school or with their families. They were middle schoolers, navigating a veritable minefield of social, personal and academic issues. She hoped the class chats gave them a forum to speak to their peers in dance and to ask advice from her as an impartial adult. She kept what the children said to her in confidence, except in instances where one of her students might be in danger. Thankfully, she hadn't run into that issue so far, so she'd built a rapport with the youngsters under her tutelage.

Eleven-year-old Marie raised her hand. "Some of the girls at school have been calling me a geek because I read comic books."

Nona shook her head. "I'm sorry to hear that, Marie. What is our motto when it comes to our interests?"

The children repeated the often-said phrase in unison. "Being me is the only way to be."

"Right." Nona sent a smile Marie's way. "So if you like comic books, keep right on reading them."

"I like comics, too." The remark came from twelve-year-old Diamond. "Maybe we can trade."

Marie's eyes lit up.

Nona smiled even brighter. "See? You got yourself a comic buddy, right here in class. Now, does anybody else have something they want to talk about?"

The question was met with silence and head shakes.

"You're sure?"

The only noise in the room was Diamond and Marie's excited comic book–related banter.

Nona clasped her hands together. "Okay. Then I have a question for you all."

Ten sets of surprised eyes looked her way.

Ralph, her oldest student at fourteen, asked, "You want our advice on something?"

She nodded. "Yes. You all know that I work as a reporter for the newspaper. I have an article to write about a man who just won a very important contract from the city."

"Okay, so what's the problem?" Diamond focused on Nona, eyes filled with questions.

"The man I'm supposed to interview is very secretive. I've spoken to him twice and still don't know very much about him. At least not enough to write my story. So what do you all think I could do to get him to tell me about himself?"

She looked around the room, taking in her students' thoughtful expressions. She hadn't intended to ask them about this when she'd come into the studio today, but she figured she didn't have anything to lose. She needed to get Ken to open up somehow if she were to have any chance of meeting her deadline.

Ralph spoke first. "What does he like to do for a hobby?"

"I know he likes to run. I went on a run with him the other day, and that helped some."

"Well, I'd see what else he likes to do. If you do what he likes to do, I bet he'll talk to you some more." Ralph folded his arms over his chest. "Yeah. That's what I'd do."

She nodded. "Thanks, Ralph."

"No problem."

Betty, the youngest of her students, spoke then. "What about cookies? Have you tried baking him cookies?"

That suggestion made her chuckle. "No, I haven't. But at this point I'm willing to try it. Maybe I'll take him some cookies the next time I interview him. Thanks, Betty."

The girl responded with a shy smile.

"I'd say be nice to him, but you're probably already doing that." Diamond tapped her chin with her index finger. "Be honest with him and let him know you're not trying to get in his business, you're just doing your job."

Nona nodded. "Good suggestion, Diamond. Anybody else?"

No one else had anything to say.

"Well, thank you all for listening, and for your helpful suggestions to my problem. Class is dismissed."

As the children got up and gathered their belongings, Nona watched over them. Through the side windows of the one-story building, she could see their parents' vehicles idling in the parking lot. She got her clipboard from her dance bag, prepared to check off names one by one as the students were picked up. Once she'd seen all her students safely off, Nona took a minute to straighten up her space, then switched off the lights and headed to her car.

Crossing the parking lot, she enjoyed the crisp breeze that blew over her, giving her momentary respite from the humid night air. Thinking back on the advice of her students, she smiled and wondered what kind of cookies she should bake for Ken.

Knowing she'd be willing to give him cookies of a much more adult nature, she shook her head and climbed into her car.

Wednesday morning, Ken strode into his office around seven. It was a bit earlier than he usually came in to work, but he wanted to get an early start on his drafting for the Grand Pearl project. He knew Nona would arrive to interview him around nine, and he wanted two hours alone in the office to work. Lynn rarely came in before nine thirty, and the two interns came in the afternoon when they were released from their college classes.

Instead of flipping the light switch, he walked across his semidark office toward the windows. The windows went from floor to ceiling, making up the entire eastern wall of his office. Once there, he turned the handle to open the vertical blinds. Sunlight flooded the space, and he took in a deep breath. Morning light always seemed to jump-start his artistic inspiration, making mornings his most productive time for the creative side of his business. He reserved afternoons for paperwork, phone calls and the other activities constituting the practical side of his work.

He faced away from the window, looking around his private office. The walls were painted in a shade of gray so muted it appeared white. His desk was glass, with chrome legs and hardware, and had no drawers. Instead, he stored all his important papers in the two silver filing cabinets occupying the south wall behind the desk. Two bookcases sat near the cabinets, storing various mementos and trinkets. Two chrome chairs with white vinyl seats sat facing the desk. On the rare occasion he had guests in his office, they occupied those chairs.

In the center of the room was his drafting table. Comprised of chrome and stainless steel with a vinyl-covered drawing surface, the table had a matching leather-topped stool for him to sit on. The drafting table was the focal point of the space, positioned in a way to take advantage of the natural light. On the north side of the room sat a seldom-used white microfiber love seat. In place of artwork on the walls, he'd hung blueprints and sketches of his past projects.

At the drafting table, he put on his headphones and connected them to his smartphone. With a playlist of some of his favorite Max Roach and Art Blakey tunes at a low volume in his ears, he picked up his charcoal pencil and started adding lines to a large piece of fresh white paper.

As he worked, his vision for the new main hall of the Grand Pearl started to come to life. He was an architect, not an interior designer, so he kept his focus on the structural elements of the space. He sketched crown molding around the area and in a different view drew out the detail of an intricate tray ceiling he thought would enhance the aesthetic appeal of the space. He didn't look up from his illustration until his smartphone vibrated on his hip.

Taking the phone from his pocket, he read the text from Nona, alerting him that she was outside his building. Setting down his pencil, he stopped his playlist and removed his headphones. He walked out of his private office, down the hall and through the reception area to the glass doors fronting his suite. Unlocking the door, he swung it open.

A second later, he watched as Nona climbed out of her black sedan. Her hair was held back from her face by a gold headband, her hazel eyes obscured by large gold-rimmed sunglasses. She wore a sleeveless orange top, paired with a tan pencil skirt that just grazed the tops of her knees. The outfit left the lower expanse of her sable legs bared to his eyes. A smile touched his lips as he watched her walk toward him, her steps sure and confident despite the pencil-thin, sky-high orange heels on her feet. Carrying a clipboard tucked under her arm, along with a small orange clutch, she walked toward him.

"Good morning." She stuck out her hand.

He took her hand and kissed it instead of shaking it. "Good morning. Welcome to Yamada Creative."

Her perfectly arched brow lifted. "You seem to be in a much better mood today."

"I am. I came in early, and I think I've finally landed

on the right design for the main hall of the Grand Pearl."
He stood back to allow her inside, then let the door
close. As she passed him, his gaze reflexively fell to
her hips, where the skirt grazed over her body. The skirt
wasn't tight, but it fit her well enough to reveal the outline of her womanly figure. He knew that if he continued to look at her this way, a physical reaction would
soon follow. He chastised his hungry eyes, reminded
himself that she'd come there for an interview, not a romantic interlude. He swallowed, dragging his eyes away
before his body revealed the desire she ignited in him.

She stopped at the reception desk, turning his way. If
she'd felt him looking at her backside, she didn't let on.
"So I guess days get started a little late around here."

He shrugged. "My assistant usually comes in before
ten. We don't get a whole lot of visitors because of the
nature of our business."

She nodded. "I'd love to see your office."

He gestured with a finger. "This way."

Walking down the short hallway, he turned right to
lead her into his office, where she executed a full turn
to take in the sights. While her attention was on his office, he was taking advantage of the full view of her
body as she spun around. In that moment, he swore his
body temperature climbed ten degrees.

"Your office is very bright and open. I can tell you
don't do clutter."

He shook his head. "I can't concentrate in a crowded
or dark space, so I made sure my office would be well
lit and sparsely decorated. Only the essentials."

She smiled, and the room seemed even brighter. "Ah.

So I've already learned something about you, and I haven't even asked any questions yet." She moved toward the love seat. "Do you mind if we sit here?"

"No, that's fine." As he followed her, he did his best to keep his eyes on where he was going and off the tempting sway of her hips.

She sat down on one of the white cushions, crossing her legs demurely. After she'd taken out her phone and set it to record, she spoke. "So, I noticed your decor. Are all these designs yours?" She gestured to the blueprints and sketches on his office walls.

Taking a seat next to her, he nodded. "Yes. The blueprint closest to my desk is my first professional job. These sketches and blueprints are like a road map of my career thus far."

"I see." She touched her chin. "Some might see the display of only your own art as conceited or self-centered."

He cocked his head to the side. "On the contrary. Seeing my work around me helps to ground me. It helps me see my growth as an artist, and it also shows me how much I still have to learn. Do you consider it a sign of my ego, Nona?"

She seemed a bit flustered at having him question her. "No. I was merely making an observation."

He wasn't sure he believed that but decided not to push the issue. "Any more questions?"

"Yes. The trophies I see displayed on your bookcases. I know you're a runner. Do you run competitively?"

He shook his head. "I run for fitness and to relax. The trophies are for my kendo wins."

Her brow crinkled. "Kendo. I've heard of it, but I'm not familiar with the intricacies."

"Kendo is a martial art, where opponents use bamboo swords to battle. The word means 'the way of the sword.' The focus is on physical and mental discipline, courage and respect."

She appeared impressed. "Sounds interesting."

In that moment, an idea struck him. He remembered Marco's complaints, as well as his vow never to spar with Ken again. "I have an idea."

"What's that?"

"Come to the gym where I do kendo. You can see me in action and get a better understanding of me. And if you're brave enough, you can learn a few moves."

A sly smile tipped up the corners of her mouth. "If I'm brave? You mean, as brave as you were earlier when you were staring at my ass?"

He blinked a few times, noting how smoothly she'd cut him off at the knee. Then and there, he knew she'd make a brilliant sparring partner. "I suppose. I hope I didn't embarrass you."

"You may have embarrassed yourself. As far as I'm concerned, as least I know you have good taste." She winked.

A tingle ran down his back. *She's flirting with me.* Now he knew he had to cross swords with her. "So, will you come to the gym?"

She laughed and stuck out her hand. "I'm game."

Chapter 6

The afternoon sun beat down on the beach, warming Nona's feet as she dug them into the sand. It wasn't how she typically spent a Thursday. Despite the feature story she currently had in the works, she'd taken the rest of the week off to celebrate her thirty-fourth birthday in the manner most appealing to her: drinks and relaxing on the beach. So there she sat in a folding chair about twenty feet from the lapping waves of the Atlantic Ocean. She wore a blue one-piece bathing suit, a matching wide-brimmed hat, dark sunglasses and a smile. To her left was a small cooler holding ice and a few chilled miniature bottles of wine.

Hadley sat to her right. She wore a bright pink bikini, a wide-brimmed straw hat, cat-eye sunglasses and a sheer floral cover-up. Hadley, eight years Nona's junior, had been an incoming freshman during Nona's senior year. Hadley was as smart as a whip, having come to college at sixteen and graduated at nineteen. Oddly enough, Hadley had been so mature that Nona hadn't thought twice about hanging out with her, despite their age difference. Since Nona had been relatively tame during college, avoiding parties, drinking and carousing in favor of working and studying, she and Hadley had been thick as thieves.

Every time Nona had doubts about the gap year she'd taken between high school and college, she reminded herself that if she hadn't taken a year off, she probably never would have met Hadley.

Popping a piece of chocolate into her mouth, Hadley sighed. "Nona, am I ever going to be able to convince you to have a birthday party, like regular people?"

She shook her head. "We both know I'm not regular people. I prefer to spend my birthday relaxing rather than getting drunk, acting a fool and waking up the next day with a colossal hangover."

Hadley pulled her shades down, letting them rest on the bridge of her nose so Nona could see her rolling her eyes. "That's what makes birthdays fun. Come on. We never did any of that stuff in college. I was too young, and you were way too straitlaced back then."

"True. But I don't necessarily think that means we missed out on anything." She took a sip from a tiny bottle of chilled merlot.

"Speak for yourself." Hadley sat back in her chair with a dramatic sigh. "Okay, at least promise me we'll throw a real party when you turn forty. That's a milestone."

Shaking her head, Nona laughed. "I'll think about it."

"Look. If you're going to be in my *Golden Girls* squad, you gotta be able to cut loose every now and again." Hadley offered a chuckle of her own.

Nona gestured around her. "Look where we are. Am I not on the beach right now, even though I'm on deadline for a feature? I'm already cutting loose."

"Not really. It's your birthday and you only took off a few days."

She couldn't deny that truth. Generally she tried to take vacation days in between assignments, but her schedule was so packed that meant she usually ended each year with unused vacation days. It was a small step, but she was still proud of herself for taking the day off, despite the large amount of work she still had left to do on her article.

"Speaking of the feature, how is that going? Were you able to get Secret Squirrel to open up yet?"

"You're too young for that reference, Hadley. Anyway, I think I'm making progress with him, but I still haven't gotten down to his core. Not yet."

Hadley drained the last of her hard lemonade. "What do you mean? Didn't you go running with him or something?"

She nodded. "I did. And I visited his office to get a feel for his process when he's working."

"And you still don't have enough information?" Her brow hitched.

"No. But I'm supposed to go to his kendo gym later this week, so hopefully he'll be chattier then."

Hadley's dark brow arched. "Nona, you see what he's doing, don't you?"

Her face scrunching in confusion, she shook her head. "What do you mean?"

"Think about it. You've been to a coffee shop with him. You've been running with him, you've been to his office and now you're talking about doing martial arts with him."

"So?"

"So, that man is running you around on purpose! He wants to see if you show an interest in his hobbies. And so far, you are playing right into his hands."

"No, I'm not. I'm just doing my job, taking whatever steps I need to take to get my story right."

"Nope. It's more than that. Didn't you tell me the other day you thought he was fine?"

She swallowed, suddenly regretting blabbing to her girlfriend. "Yes. I did say that, but…"

"It's all good, girl. Get down with the swirl, I'm not judging. All I'm saying is you need to admit that you wouldn't be doing all this stuff with him if you weren't attracted to him."

Nona pulled the brim of her hat low over her face as she cringed. "Come on, Hadley."

"Come on, nothing. Think about the hardest interview subject you've ever had, and what you did to get the scoop. Have you ever made this much effort before?"

Running through the tougher characters she'd covered over her years working at the newspaper, she already knew who had made her work the hardest before Ken—a reclusive elderly woman who had given most of her wealth to charity and had insisted Nona help her in the garden if she wanted any information. As much as she hated to admit it, Hadley was right on both counts. No one had ever made her go through this much to get information, and if she were honest, she probably wouldn't have done it with anyone else.

"Mmm-hmm." Hadley folded her arms over her chest. "You've gotten quiet, which means you know I'm right. If Ken Yamada had a face for radio, there ain't no way you'd be participating in this gantlet of activities he's given you."

Nona smeared a hand over her face and took another sip of wine. "Crap."

Hadley merely smirked in her direction.

"Enough about me. You're the one with the exciting life on the Crystal Coast. Who are you dating right now?"

"Nice segue." Hadley stuck out her tongue. "For your information, I'm not dating anyone, thanks to my brothers."

"So I'm guessing Campbell and Savion are still on that overprotective kick, eh?"

"Girl, I don't know if they'll ever let it go." She shifted in her seat. "No man can get within thirty yards of me before they start hounding him and giving him the third degree."

"You know it's just because they love you and don't think anyone is good enough for their precious baby sister."

"Whatever. I think they're in cahoots with Daddy to keep me single and pure until I'm thirty."

Nona laughed at that, because she knew the good ship Purity had already sailed for Hadley. "What they don't know won't hurt them, right?"

"Right. I can't have them knowing all of my business. Besides, celibacy's got to count for something."

Grabbing her magazine from the sand next to her, Nona used it to fan herself, stirring up the warm, humid air encircling her. Looking out on the surface of the water, she thought about what Hadley had pointed out. Was this really about her story? Or was she letting Ken drag her all over the Queen City because she found him irresistible?

Either way, she was in too deep now to change her strategy. And with less than two weeks before her article was due, she didn't have the luxury of stepping back.

She had to find out who Ken really was, both for the sake of her feature and for her own purposes.

When Ken visited his father's home for dinner Friday evening, he let himself into the house with his spare key. As usual, the house was mostly dark and quiet. Walking through the grand foyer, Ken once again wondered why his father insisted on clinging to this house. It was much too large for a man of his age, especially one who lived alone. Beyond that, Ken knew the house held many painful memories for his father, and he couldn't figure out why he'd want to face those old ghosts every day.

Months ago, Ken had tried to have yet another conversation with his father about selling the house and moving into something smaller and more manageable. The conversation had quickly gone downhill, with the old man ranting about how this was his home and he had no intention of leaving it as long as he lived. There had been nothing he could say to convince the old man to leave the house, so Ken had let the matter drop, hoping to revisit it later.

While he made his way to the dining room, Ken noted how cavernous the house seemed these days. He'd grown up here, and by most standards, it was a modest family home. With four bedrooms and three bathrooms, it had had just enough space for the family's needs back then. But now, with the three thousand square feet being occupied only by one frail old man, an echoing emptiness filled the place.

He walked farther down the hall, headed toward the light flooding from the dining room. Just outside the door, he stopped at the side table and picked up a small silver-framed portrait. The image of the smiling, youthful woman, her stomach swollen with child, was one of his favorite pictures of his late mother. He knew from the stories his parents had told him that the photograph had been taken while she was pregnant with Ken, as she and his father enjoyed a day in the park. It was also one of the few portraits his father had kept after his mother's untimely death.

A slight smile touched his lips as he remembered her quiet, loving nature. Setting the photo back in its place, he entered the dining room.

Inside, he found his father sitting in his usual spot

at the head of the low black-lacquered table. "Hello, Father."

"Hello, son. Come in." From his seat on the cushion, Hiro Yamada motioned to him.

Sitting in his usual spot to his father's right, Ken bowed. The food for the evening had already been laid out by Hiro's housekeeper, Frances Crane. Over the years she'd worked for the family, she'd become very adept at Japanese cooking. The grilled meats, jasmine rice and sautéed vegetables she'd prepared perfumed the air with a delicious aroma.

As Ken and Hiro ate, the dining room remained mostly silent. Ken watched his father discreetly, noting the careful way he ate. The old man guided each bite to his mouth with a slow hand. Despite his efforts to hide it, Ken could clearly see the tremor in his movements.

"Father. Are you sure you have all the help you need? Because there is more that can be done."

Looking up from his plate of food, Hiro offered a long sigh. "Son, I am fine. I'm not as young as I used to be, but I can still take care of myself. Stop pestering me."

He smiled in spite of his father's sour mood, knowing that was simply the old man's way. "I worry about you because I love you, Father."

"You love me so much? Then let's talk of something else."

Shaking his head, Ken took a sip of tea, then did as his father wished. "I told you about the Grand Pearl Theater project. Now the *Observer* has assigned a reporter to write a feature article on me."

Hiro set his chopsticks aside. "Really? And how much have you told this reporter?"

"So far, not much. She knows about my running, my kendo—"

"She?" The old man's eyes were locked on him.

"Yes. The reporter is a woman. Her name is Nona Gregory, and she—"

"Has my name come up?"

Ken could tell his father was agitated, by both his tone and his repeated interruptions. "Yes. She asked if we were related, but I refused to answer."

Hiro responded with a slow shake of his head. "If she is a reporter, she will find out. It's only a matter of time before she does."

"Don't worry. Everything will be fine. After all, the story is about me, not you."

"It doesn't matter, son. Once the connection is made, she will latch on to the scandal of our past." His eyes changed then, becoming empty, unseeing. "Soon the secret shame of this family will be made public."

Ken sighed. While he understood his father's concerns, he didn't like the way he was talking. "Miyu is not shameful, Father. I love her."

"I care for her as well." His eyes remained devoid of emotion. "But the circumstances of her birth are shameful to our family legacy."

Ken pushed his plate away, his appetite gone. He said nothing, knowing his words wouldn't matter. Hiro was well past the age when a man made up his mind about certain things, and he couldn't be convinced otherwise.

"Son, all I ask is that you give me as much time as

you can, stall her somehow. If my secrets are going to come out, I need time to prepare."

Even though he wasn't sure how much he could do, Ken nodded. "I promise, Father. I will do what I can."

The old man leaned back, his shoulders slumping. In that moment, his face and body language showed every one of the seventy-nine years he'd lived. "I worked hard as commissioner to give the people a good life. Perhaps too hard."

Ken's heart twisted in his chest, because he knew exactly what his father meant.

"I'm old, weary. I have so little fight left in me. But what I have, I will give to protect our family name." A tiny spark lit his eyes, and he sat a bit straighter, resolute in his declaration.

Ken reached out, placed a hand on his father's thin shoulder. "So will I."

Chapter 7

Nona slowly swung open the door of Satori Martial Arts Saturday, then stepped inside. The space before her was wide and open, even cavernous. The wooden floor felt firm yet springy beneath her feet. The east and west walls were mirrored, reflecting the movements of the five or six people who were practicing various martial arts in different sections of the room. All of the people present wore the white outfits and colored sashes traditionally associated with karate, tae kwon do and the like. Looking down at her black sneakers, yoga pants and tee, she felt somewhat out of place.

Chuckling to herself, she admitted that her outfit was the least of her concern. In a few minutes, she'd be facing an interview subject holding a wooden sword. Her energies were best spent figuring out how not to get hurt in the process. Hadley had been right. This was by far the most work she'd ever had to do to get a story.

She saw a short-legged wooden bench near the door. Not wanting to wander around the gym looking lost, she dropped down onto the seat to wait for Ken. While she waited, watching the people performing their moves, she thought about the questions she had for Ken. She still didn't know much about how he got started in the arts or what inspired him. She was determined to find out the answers to those questions tonight. It would be the least he could do in exchange for asking her to step so far outside her comfort zone.

"Hi, Nona."

The deep, familiar timbre of Ken's voice drew Nona out of her thoughts and back into reality. Looking up, she saw him standing before her, shirtless. "Hello, Ken." Getting the words out was quite a feat, as most of her concentration disappeared when she took in the sight of his muscular torso and arms.

"Are you ready to try your hand at kendo?" His smile was easy, and his dark eyes held a twinkle of mischief.

"As ready as I'm going to get."

He extended a hand to help her up, and she took it. As his large hand closed over her smaller one, she felt a tingle of electricity travel down her spine. Once she was on her feet, she continued to stand there, staring at him.

A few moments passed between them in silence as they assessed each other.

Her heart thudded loudly in her ears. Searching the depths of his sparkling dark eyes, she felt as if she were a small animal ensnared in a trap. Her curiosity, combined with her inexplicable physical attraction to him, had a serious hold on her.

Finally, he released his grip on her hand. "Follow me. It's this way."

She stayed close to him as he moved down a short corridor and into a room on the left. This space looked nearly identical to the main room of the gym but was about a third of the size. Unlike the main room, there was no one else present. "Are we going to be alone for this?"

He nodded. "It's safer that way. Kendo takes up a good amount of space, and having other people in here makes it more likely someone will get hurt."

She smiled to communicate her understanding. As he moved past her, she stood near the door and awaited further instruction. This was her first foray into martial arts and, hopefully, her ticket into Ken's inner workings. Watching his shirtless, muscular frame move around the space, it occurred to her that he had become a delectable riddle, an irresistible puzzle she was determined to solve.

He gave her a brief description of the usual procedures of the sport. "Kendo always begins with a bow." He bowed to her.

She mimicked him.

"You would usually be taught etiquette now. But I don't want to overwhelm you, so I'll keep it brief. Basically, you must enter the dojo with no malice or negativity in your heart. Respect and discipline are your main goals. Remember that and you'll be golden." Then he chose two *bokuto*, bamboo practice swords, from a wall-mounted rack near the back of the room. Walking back over to where she stood, he handed one to her.

She took it, squeezed the hilt. "Okay. Go easy on me, because I have no idea what I'm doing."

He smiled while he made his way to the center of the room. He adjusted his stance and waited for her to mimic him. "Of course. I wouldn't dream of hurting you, Nona."

She could hear the sincerity in his voice, and her instincts told her she could trust him. Matching his position, she readied her sword. "Maybe my dance skills will come in handy here."

In response to her verbal musing, he asked, "Dance?"

She nodded. "I teach an intermediate jazz dance class a couple of nights each week."

He appeared impressed. "So now I've learned something about you."

"We're not going to actually fight, are we?" She held her sword with the business end pointed at the floor.

"No. I'm just going to show you a few basic moves. After that, you can ask me a few questions."

"A few? Is that more than three?"

"It's at least four," he teased, winking at her.

She couldn't hold back her grin. In a normal interview situation, she liked her interview subjects to be far more forthcoming than he'd been. Somehow, though, she'd begun to enjoy the paces he was putting her through.

Over the next half hour, Ken walked her through five basic kendo moves. He kept his movements slow, allowing her to observe him, then stepped back and indicated she should mimic him. It had been so long since her days as a student, and that gave her an odd feeling throughout the lesson. *I guess this is what the kids in my class experience.* He was a patient, dedicated teacher, and that was the way she hoped her students perceived her.

Watching his fluid, skillful movements, she couldn't help thinking that she'd never been lucky enough to have a teacher quite this attractive before. His muscles flexed and contracted in time with his gestures, making it hard for her to concentrate on what he attempted to teach her. But she managed to get it together, and by the time he was done, he appeared pleased with her efforts.

"That was actually pretty good for a first timer." He took their bamboo swords back to the wall rack and replaced them in their slots. "You'll be ready to spar for real in no time."

"If you say so." She followed him to the bench near the door, and the two of them sat down.

Their thighs brushed together. Even though the contact was brief, and layers of fabric separated them, it was still enough to make her jump as a tiny current of awareness shot through her.

He scooted over a bit, breaking the contact. "Sorry. Didn't mean to get so close."

I liked it. So help her, she liked it. But she had better sense than to give voice to that thought. Letting what she hoped was a casual smile show on her face, she waved it off. "No biggie."

"Do you think you'd enjoy learning more about

kendo? Because I think you have some natural talent for it."

Her brow hitched. "Really? I felt pretty awkward out there."

"That's typical for a first timer. But I think you were right. Your command of dance does give you an advantage."

Of all the things she'd expected to hear tonight, that certainly wasn't one of them. She cupped her chin, considering his words.

"If you decide you want to learn more, you can always come here. I don't officially teach, but I'm willing to tutor a promising student like you." A confident smile lit his face as his eyes swept over her.

Heat rose into her cheeks, and she knew she'd better steer the conversation toward her interview before she forgot herself completely and did something stupid. "Thanks, I'll think about it. But I'd really like to get to my questions."

"Sure." He stood, stretched his arms over his head. "Let me get into a clean shirt and we can talk in the snack bar."

Ken sat across from Nona at a small table in the snack bar, watching her over his strawberry-kiwi protein smoothie. She was riffling through her purse, searching for her smartphone so she could record their words…again. He sipped from his plastic cup, slumped back in his chair. He knew that once she found her phone, she'd have plenty of questions for him.

Mindful of the conversation he'd had with his father, he mentally prepared himself for the barrage he anticipated. Nona's savvy had been apparent from his very first encounter with her, so he assumed she'd already identified him as Hiro Yamada's son. In keeping with the promise he'd made to his father, Ken decided he'd play his cards close to his chest. He'd let her talk, find out exactly how much she knew, then answer her questions accordingly.

He'd finished a third of his smoothie by the time she finally dug up her phone. After she'd activated the recording app and set the gadget in the center of the table, she turned her eyes his way. "Sorry about that. Now, I'd like to start the interview by asking you about your craft. What initially sparked your interest in art and architecture?"

He smiled. "Right to the point."

She matched his smile. "This *is* our fourth interview, Ken."

He noticed how casually she referred to him by his first name. The knowledge that she felt comfortable with him gave him a modicum of pleasure. "My interest in art began with my late mother, Aiko. She was a very talented sketch artist, working in charcoal and sometimes pastels. From a very young age, I can remember sitting on her lap as she sketched. Her passion for drawing was evident, and it rubbed off on me." The familiar twinge of emotion hit him, as it always did when he spoke of his mother. He'd loved her dearly, and carried her memory in his heart every day.

Nodding, Nona sipped from her own berry smoothie before responding. "Is your mother the same Aiko Yamada who taught Advanced Drawing Technique at the Carolina Institute of Art?"

His brow hitched, while a series of prickles ran down his back. "Yes. I can see you've been doing your research."

"I have. I also know that during her tenure at the institute, Professor Yamada was very well respected by both her students and her colleagues. There are still pieces of hers hanging on the walls of the administrative and classroom buildings on campus, some thirty-five years after she stopped teaching there."

He rested his chin on his fist. Even he hadn't known about that, and he made a mental note to visit the college when he had a chance, to see which of his mother's pieces were on display. "This will probably be a nice extra tidbit of information, but my most prized possession is a portrait my mother sketched of me when I was four years old. It's on my living room wall at home."

"Thank you for sharing that. And you're right, extra things like that do help to enrich my stories." She leaned forward, resting her elbows on the tabletop. "You understand that I've made the connection between you and both of your parents, correct?"

He released a long exhale. As his father had said, any real reporter would make the connection, and she'd done it almost immediately. "Yes. I'm sure you know that former commissioner Yamada is my father."

"Yes. I would ask you why you tried to conceal that from me, but I'm sure that wouldn't yield much in terms of positive results or information."

He felt his jaw tighten slightly. "It wouldn't."

She clasped her hands together. "So you don't have anything to say pertaining to your parents?"

"I've already spoken about my mother. As for my father, all I will say is that he is the person who inspired my love of architecture."

"That's a start."

"As far back as I can recall, Dad collected books on architecture, built miniature models of famous landmarks and took me to see buildings under construction. It's totally unrelated to politics, and I think that was why he loved it so much."

She fixed him with a penetrating stare. "Is there anything more I should know about your father and your relationship with him, then and now?"

He sensed her delving, trying to get beneath the surface of what he was telling her. But he was a private man, and he wasn't about to turn over the entire details of his personal life to her, no matter how attractive he found her. "Yes. He also inspired my love of jazz music. He played Max Roach, Art Blakey, Coltrane, the works. That led me to my third hobby—"

"Playing the drums for the Queen City Gents jazz quartet." She completed his sentence, as if it were natural for her to do so.

Usually it annoyed him when he felt someone getting too close to him, digging into his life. But there was something about Nona that tempered his reaction. Instead of being irritated with her, he felt somewhat impressed. "You're putting in quite a lot of effort to find out about me. I'm not sure you even need me anymore." He let the humor he felt seep into his tone.

She rolled her eyes, but her smile remained bright and beautiful. "You flatter me, Ken. It's my job to know as much as I can about you. I do the same thing with all my interview subjects."

Draining his smoothie, he looked into her eyes. "Really. How many of your subjects have you gone running with? Or done martial arts with?"

She blinked, then her gaze fled from his. "None. You're the first."

He adjusted his expression, hoping to indicate how he felt about the double meaning of her words.

Her eyes grew wide, and she sat straight up in her chair as realization hit her. She hit the button on her phone to cease the recording. "Wait. I didn't mean it like that. I meant…well, you know what I meant." She looked flustered, even a bit embarrassed.

It was a big change from the put-together, confident woman he'd come to know, but parts of him enjoyed seeing her a bit off her game. "However you meant it, I'm not against being your first."

Her eyes rose slowly to meet his. "Ken."

"It's true." He shrugged his shoulders, ready to level with her. She'd gotten closer to him than any other woman during his entire adult life, so he saw no reason to keep hiding his growing attraction to her. As things stood, he didn't see his fascination with her going away any time soon.

She ran a hand over her hair, tugged at the end of her ponytail. "You haven't made it easy for me to find out who you really are."

"I know. But you never backed down, and I respect

that." He was out of his seat by the time he finished his sentence.

Her eyes tracked him as he entered her space, but she made no effort to move away. "I'm…drawn to you. I know part of it is journalistic curiosity, but there's something else there."

"Attraction?" He bent at the waist, bringing his face level with hers.

The tip of her tongue darted out to wet her lower lip. "Yes."

Enticed by her admission, her fragrance and the expression of wonder on her face, he reached out to cup her chin.

Tilting her face up, he placed his lips gently against hers. A soft sigh escaped her as he kissed her, letting the tip of his tongue stroke against the soft petal of her lower lip before slipping into her mouth. She tasted of berries, combined with a delectable sweetness he knew was unique to her. Claiming her mouth made heat fill his body and sent blood rushing to fill lower parts of his anatomy.

The kiss continued until she tensed, then broke the seal of their lips. When he looked at her, he could see the confusion playing across her features.

"Are you okay?" He wanted to know if he'd done something wrong or made her feel uncomfortable.

She drew in a deep breath. "It's nothing. But it's late, and I should get home."

He stood, stepped back to allow her the space she needed. Rising from her seat, she gathered her phone and purse. The remnants of passion on her face were soon replaced with her professional mask.

"Thank you for answering my questions. I'll be in touch." She slung the purse strap over her shoulder. "Good night, Ken."

"Good night." By the time he got the word out, she was already walking away. Her strides were long, and soon she was out of sight.

Ken stood by the table for a few long moments, wondering what had just happened between them. With no answers to that question, he tossed their empty plastic cups in the recycling bin and went to retrieve his gym bag.

There's just no understanding women.

Chapter 8

Sunday evening, Nona parked her car in the driveway of her parents' home. The two-story house in a quiet northern nook of University City had been her family home since her teen years. She got out of her car, went to the front door and found it already unlocked. Her parents were expecting her, but when she stepped inside, she didn't see either of them in the living room.

"Mommy? Daddy? It's me!" she called out for her parents, then listened for a reply.

Instead, she heard a soft giggle, one she knew belonged to her mother. The sound floated down from upstairs. Shaking her head, she plopped down on the sofa. Her parents had been married thirty-five years but were still prone to hormone-driven interludes that belied their age and their long marriage. After one too many awkward moments, she'd learned not to go searching the house for them. There was no telling what they might be doing—or how many articles of clothing they'd be wearing. So rather than risk seeing something she couldn't unsee, she grabbed the remote and flipped on the television. That way they would know she was there and could come down when they were ready.

By the time her mother's slipper-clad feet appeared on the stairs, Nona had settled into both the couch and an old rerun of *Law and Order.* "Hey, Mommy. Where's Daddy?"

Descending to the floor, Aretha Raines Gregory tightened the belt of her blue floral silk robe. "Your daddy will be down in a few. How have you been, baby?"

"Pretty good. Got a feature at work, so that's been taking up most of my time lately."

Aretha smiled, easing over and taking a seat on the sofa next to her only child. "Really? In your section or on the main page?"

"Main page."

"That's great news. I'm telling you, if you stay on the right path, you'll be editor in chief in a few years." Aretha stifled a yawn. "Just imagine it. My baby as editor in chief of the *Charlotte Observer.* Wouldn't that be something?"

"Yeah, Mommy. It would." She didn't mention to her mother that her feelings about her work at the paper had changed over the years. There had been a time, when she'd been in her twenties and filled with youthful zeal, that she would have been thrilled to take on the editor-in-chief position. Back then, she'd wanted to take over the world, starting with the newspaper. But now, as she headed toward her midthirties, she found that she didn't get the same thrill out of getting the scoop, breaking the story or seeing her name in the byline.

Gordon Gregory walked in the room then. Dressed in a red T-shirt and a pair of cargo pants, he shuffled toward his favorite spot on the love seat facing the television. "Hey, Nonie. How are you?"

"Fine, Daddy. How are you?"

"Pretty good." He eased into his seat. "School's out, so I'm on easy street."

She shook her head. As much as her father complained about the students during the school year, everyone knew he loved his work as a librarian in the J. Murrey Atkins Library at the University of North Carolina at Charlotte.

Both her parents worked at the college, which was why they'd chosen to make their home in University City. Her mother, an assistant professor of journalism, had been Nona's biggest advocate when she'd decided to pursue journalism as a career. Nona hadn't gone to UNC Charlotte, choosing to attend school at North Carolina A&T. At eighteen, she hadn't relished the idea of seeing her parents on campus every day.

Ever supportive, her parents hadn't made a fuss about her choice of school and had sent her off to Greensboro with their best wishes. Aretha hadn't been so thrilled about her daughter minoring in dance, but she'd let it go once she realized Nona wasn't going to change her mind.

."Honey, Nona got a feature article. Front page!" Aretha gestured excitedly as she communicated the news to her husband.

"Wonderful. I'm sure you'll do great, Nonie. When is the story due?"

"I've got about a few days left to get it done." She half watched the images playing across the television screen as she spoke.

Gordon nodded. "What's it about?"

"Yes, tell us. Did you get an interesting subject to cover for your first front-page feature?" Aretha leaned in, waiting for her answer.

Taking her eyes off the television to offer her parents her full focus, Nona explained the scope of the story. "Basically, I'm supposed to give the readers a peek into who Ken is, a look at his process and a preview of his vision for the Grand Pearl."

Aretha folded her arms across her chest. "Ken? You've just met him and you're so informal with him already?"

She cast a sidelong glance in her mother's direction. "He asked me to call him by his first name. Besides, we've had four interviews, so I think we're past the formal stage."

Now Aretha's face scrunched into a frown. "*Four* interviews? I don't think I've ever known you to interview someone more than twice. What exactly is going on between you and this man?"

"Oh, come on now, Rethie." Having settled comfortably into his seat, Gordon scoffed at his wife. "Stop giving her the third degree."

"Gordon, I know my little girl. If she's seen him that many times already, there must be something going on."

Nona interjected. "Mommy, I don't want you to worry. Ken is an artist, and you know how eccentric they can be. I just have to dig a little deeper with him, that's all. It will all pay off when I write a fabulous feature."

"Humph." Aretha didn't appear convinced.

Nona looked to her father and found him studying her. "What is it, Daddy?"

"Nonie, is there something going on between you and this Ken person? I can't help but notice the way your expression changed when you started talking about him."

She let her gaze drop. "He is attractive, and I..."

"See?" Aretha jerked her head in Nona's direction. "I knew it."

"Mommy, Daddy, the truth is there's a mutual attraction between us. But we're keeping things very professional." She preferred to be honest with her parents when she could, at least to a point. For instance, she saw no reason they should know that Ken had kissed her, twice, and she'd made no effort to stop him.

"So far." Her mother sat back on the sofa, sinking into the gray suede cushion. "Don't let whatever is going on between you ruin your career, baby. There is such a thing as journalistic integrity."

"I know, Mommy. I promise to keep things on the professional level." Nona knew all about what her mother was hinting at, and she hoped agreeing with her right away might prevent her from launching into a long, tedious lecture.

"I trust you, Nonie. I'm sure you'll use your good judgment." Her father's words were quiet, but firm.

"Thanks, Daddy." She appreciated his vote of confidence. Her father had always been the more laid-back parent, while her mother thrived on order and practicality. Thinking it was well past time for a change of subject, she announced, "I forgot to tell you. My dance students have mastered their basic turns. I think they're going to do very well in their recital next month."

Aretha's face twisted into another frown. "Oh, Nona. Are you still teaching those little critters? You know that time would be better spent on things related to your *real* career, don't you?"

While she wanted to roll her eyes, Nona knew better. "Mommy, I'm not going to stop teaching. I love dance, and I love seeing what a difference it makes in the lives of my kids."

"Ugh. *Your* kids." Aretha threw up her hands. "That's another thing you could be pursuing if you weren't teaching over there—a husband and some grandbabies for me."

Nona let her head drop back against the cushion behind her, blowing out an exasperated breath. She'd been hearing about her mother's desire for grandchildren since she was twenty-one. Having been down this road many times before, she gave the only acceptable response. "I know, Mommy. I know."

Gordon's chuckle broke through their tense exchange. "If you want grandkids so bad, why are you trying to stop her from dating the guy she's interviewing? How do you expect her to get pregnant if all she does is bury herself under work?" He laughed again as he finished his question.

Nona shook her head as a chuckle erupted from her mouth. "Daddy!"

Aretha pursed her lips, but the humor was apparent in her eyes. "Oh, hush up, Gordon."

Laughing, Nona looked between her parents. They were quite a pair, but they kept life interesting for her at every turn.

Ken sat by the window in the Charlotte Plaza Starbucks on Friday evening, flipping through the pages of *Architectural Digest.* He was expecting Nona any moment for what she'd said would be their final interview. He had mixed feelings about that, because while he didn't want to monopolize all her time, he also wasn't ready to have her disappear from his life. Over the past two weeks, he'd already become accustomed to having her around.

He remembered how annoyed she'd been with him when he showed up late for their first interview, so he'd made sure to arrive a little early this time. He wasn't one to be rude, but he also wouldn't change his entire schedule for the convenience of another person, either. Something about Nona had him doing all kinds of things he'd never done before.

When she walked through the door of the coffee shop, his gaze went to her immediately. She wore her hair in a low bun, revealing the soft lines of her face. Her body was draped in a bright blue maxi dress with thin straps. The dress covered most of the lithe form beneath but left her neck, shoulders and arms bare to his appreciative eyes. A pair of blue crystal earrings dangled from her lobes, brushing against her shoulders as she walked.

She looked around for a moment, and he raised his hand to wave her toward him. Her attention swung his way as she spotted him. Watching her approach, he took a draw from his iced coffee to cool off. Whenever she entered his space, a rising heat accompanied her. His awareness of the heat crackling between them was such that he'd forgone his usual hot beverage for something on ice.

She slid into the seat across from him with a soft smile on her face. "Thanks for meeting me again. I hope this will be the last time I have to pump you for information."

He chuckled. "We'll see. I'm trying to give you what you need, but telling my life story isn't exactly easy for me. I don't know if you can tell, but I'm a pretty private person."

She placed a hand to her chest, her eyes wide with mock surprise. "Heavens, I had no idea! You've been so chatty up until now."

Shaking his head, he took another drink of the cool, rich brew in his cup. "So, what's missing from your story?"

"I've filled in most of the basics, either from our previous interviews or from my own independent research." She pulled out her phone, and after a bit of swiping, began rattling off information. "I know you graduated from the Carolina Institute of Art with your bachelor of fine arts, and then received your dual master's in architecture and urban design from UNC Charlotte. It's possible you met my parents—they both work at UNC Charlotte."

He scratched his chin as he accessed the memories. "There was a librarian that had the last name Gregory. Is he your dad?"

She nodded. "Probably. As far as I know he's the only Gregory at the library. My mother teaches in the journalism department, so you were less likely to have run into her."

"No, I don't think I did. I never took any classes in that department."

"Okay. I also know about the accident that widowed your father. My condolences, by the way."

"Thank you." He tried to ignore the tightening in his chest and hoped she would change the subject.

"I'm sure my boss would love for me to press you about the details of that accident, because the records are sealed and things are quite muddy. But the story isn't about your parents. It's about you."

He couldn't put his relief into words, but he tried. "I really appreciate that you realize that."

She shrugged. "He knows I'm going to do my story my way or not at all. So what I'd really like to talk about now is your process and what inspires you while you work."

"I listen to jazz while I sketch, if that's what you mean. You already know I love to work in morning light and that I need a clean, clutter-free space."

"Do you have a favorite jazz artist? Someone you

listen to often, whose work has informed yours more than anyone else?"

"Definitely Max Roach. When I drum for the band, I'm mainly emulating his style. The man's a genius on the drums."

She cocked her head to one side. "I'm not familiar with him."

"Do you listen to jazz?"

"Yes, but it's more contemporary, smooth jazz. I love Joyce Cooling and Boney James."

"Well, all the smooth jazz artists of the present owe their craft to the greats like Max Roach, to some degree. Their pioneering work formed the basis of jazz as it is today." He could feel his passion for the music rising. "I probably would never have picked up drumming if it wasn't for Max."

She nodded. "I can sense your passion right now. You seem to be equally ardent about all your pursuits— your work, kendo, running and now drumming. How can that be?"

"Simple." He rested his elbows on the tabletop, leaning in as he laced his fingers together. "I believe in only doing the things that inspire passion within. If I don't feel strongly about a thing…or a person, I don't pursue it."

Her gaze shifted, making a direct connection with his. "When is the last time you felt passionately about a person?"

He held her gaze. "When I walked into this coffee shop that day and saw you."

Her sharp intake of breath conveyed her surprise.

Her cheeks bloomed with red. "Ken, I don't know what to say."

"You don't have to say anything." He reached across the table to capture her hand. "It's obvious what's happening between us."

With a soft sigh, she admitted, "You're right. There's definitely something between us. I mean, I have what I need for my story. But I still want to see you again."

A grin broke out over his face when he heard that. "Looks like we agree on that."

"You know what's funny? I was at my parents' house last night, and my mom chewed me out about journalistic integrity when she found out I was attracted to you."

He chuckled. "And how did she know that?"

"She sensed it. Moms are very intuitive, or at least my mother is. After she figured it out, I had no choice but to admit it."

The idea of that amused him. "And how does your dad feel about the matter?"

"He's way more laid-back than Mommy, so he's cool. He actually joked that she should quit fussing at me and let me date you so she could maybe get some grandchildren out of the deal."

He put up his free hand in mock defense. "Hold on now. I like you, but I don't know about all this."

She rolled her eyes, her expression playful. "Quit it. I'm not jumping that far ahead yet. But I would like to spend some more time with you, see where this thing goes."

That was easily the best thing he'd heard all day. "Sounds good. What are you doing Wednesday night?"

"Nothing after work. I teach my dance class Tuesday and Thursday, so I'm free."

"Cool. We'll get together then, at Satori. You game for some more kendo, and maybe dinner?"

She looked a bit nervous. "I guess, as long as you promise to keep going easy on me."

Giving her hand a squeeze, he smiled. "On the kendo floor, I will. But I won't go easy on you when it comes to winning your heart."

In response, she leaned forward and grabbed his free hand. "I wouldn't want you to."

He shifted his upper body, and their lips connected for a sweet, lingering kiss.

Chapter 9

Nona spent Monday morning pulling together her notes to build the basis for her article draft. She felt she'd spent enough time with Ken, questioning and observing him, to allow her to give an accurate portrayal of who he was and how he went about his job. As a complement to her work with him, she'd contacted the city planning department and spoken with a few members of the committee who'd chosen Ken's proposal from among those submitted.

All three of the people from the city had deemed Ken's proposal innovative, which had been one of the top priorities given to the committee in making their decision.

"Mr. Yamada's design proposal was simply amazing," committee member Mary Kearns said in an email.

"In terms of being respectful of the historical significance of the Grand Pearl Theater, while still updating it to modern standards, we didn't see any other design that even came close."

"I was amazed with Mr. Yamada's immense respect for the project and for the city's funds. That respect was literally written into the proposal's wording, but when he came in to deliver his pitch in person during the second phase of bidding, it was made even clearer to us." That quote came from Mitchell Davis, another committee member, via a voice mail he'd left Nona over the weekend.

During her chat with Nona by phone, committee chair Debra Velez heaped more praise on Ken and his design. "Mr. Yamada definitely gave us the best design, with the freshest ideas. Beyond that, his bid was very reasonable. He didn't request an extravagant amount that would bankrupt the city's discretionary fund, yet he didn't lowball us in a way that might make us suspect shoddy work. We could tell he understood the scope and the importance of the project and genuinely wanted to be a part of it."

By the time Nona finished chatting with Mrs. Velez, even she was impressed. She could tell that Ken had won over the committee on pure merit. Mrs. Velez had promised to send Nona a copy of Ken's winning proposal, and she expected it to arrive in her email inbox later in the day. That would be the final piece to complete the basis of her story.

At lunchtime, Nona ordered in so she could remain at her desk. She often took working lunches when she had an important story to write, and this one seemed to be taking on a life of its own. Between bites of her grilled chicken salad, she typed up the first draft of her article. Like most of her drafts, it was more outline than prose. She laid out the basic structure of the feature, placing her thoughts in an abbreviated form that she'd go back and expand on later. This bare-bones layout would provide the framework on which she'd build the article, breathing life and character into it before sending it off to her editor.

As the two o'clock hour rolled around, Nona got up from her desk to stretch. She left her office with her favorite mug in hand, passing the cubicles in the general press pool on her way to the break room. There was no one else in the room, so she went straight for the coffee machine to make herself a cup. After spending the last couple of hours working on her article, she was a bit bleary-eyed.

While her afternoon pick-me-up brewed, she inhaled the deep, rich scent. When it was done, she grabbed her Daffy Duck mug from the tray. She added a little cream and sweetener, then carried the mug out of the room, intent on returning to her desk.

She passed Huff's office and stopped when she heard the sound of someone sobbing. His door was not completely closed, letting the sound escape through the small opening.

What's going on in there? The sob had sounded female, so she had to assume it wasn't her boss who was crying. Usually she tried not to be nosy, but if someone was hurt, maybe she could help.

She peered through the space between the door and the frame and saw Casey Dunning slumped in a chair in front of Wendell's desk.

"I'm sorry, Casey," she heard Wendell say. "But the higher-ups are making cuts. There wasn't anything more I could do."

Casey's answer to that came in the form of another sob.

Oh, no. Backing away from the door, Nona turned away. By then, she could see quite a few curious sets of eyes directed toward the office door. Some people were even peering over or around their cubicle partitions to see what was going on.

Shaking her head, Nona hurried off to return to her office. There, she left her door open and returned to her seat behind her own desk. Sipping from the mug of coffee, she felt a sense of dread wash over her. Morale at the paper was an important factor, one that determined the quality of their editorial. Once word of staff cuts started to travel around the office, which would likely happen at any moment, the dynamic would shift, upsetting the precarious balance of the work environment.

While Casey sometimes got on her nerves, Nona would never have wished anything like this on her. Aside from that, knowing that the executive staff was making cutbacks made her nervous about the security of her own position. She'd been with the paper since college, over a decade. Still, that wouldn't save her job from the chopping block if she were suddenly deemed expendable.

She went back to her work, trying to push what she'd

seen out of her mind. All that went out the window when she looked up and saw Casey, her face still wet with tears, trudging past her office door. In her arms was the telltale cardboard box, holding all the things that had once occupied Casey's desk. Casey had been with the paper for two years, and Nona wouldn't have dreamed she would be leaving this way. While a little goofy at times, Casey had always been judicious about her work.

Casey stopped, poking her head in the door. "See you around, Nona." Her tone held resignation, defeat.

"I wish you all the best, Casey." It was the truth, and the only thing she could think to say.

With a solemn nod, Casey moved on.

Nona knew if she spun her chair around, she would see Casey in the parking lot, loading her belongings into her car. So she kept her attention on her computer screen, hoping to take her focus off the unfortunate situation, since she had no control over it.

Wendell tapped on her office door a few minutes later. "Nona, got a minute?"

Looking up, she ceased her typing. "Sure thing, Huff. Come on in."

He entered, sitting down in her guest chair. "I'm assuming you know by now that we had to let Casey go."

She nodded. "Yeah. Just gave her my best."

"It's a damn shame. But my hands are tied on this one. Subscriptions are down, and the suits are getting nervous. They're looking to cut costs however they can."

"I know." She'd been hearing varying versions of this

story for the past five or six years. As more and more people sought their news online, print publications of all types suffered. Newspapers were among the hardest hit by the shift in the way people accessed the news.

"Since we had to cut Casey from your staff, we're going to have to add her workload to yours. Hopefully you'll be able to handle it."

She sighed. "Couldn't Rick or Crystal take over some of it?" They were now her two remaining reporters.

He shook his head. "Rick's doing double duty for sports, and Crystal's been cut back to part-time. So you're going to have to pick up the slack. Can you do it?"

"I can't say I'm thrilled about it, but I'll make it work." She ran a hand through her hair, feeling the pressure rising within her.

"Thanks, Nona. You know I appreciate it."

"I don't suppose this comes with a raise," she asked wryly, already knowing the answer.

"I'll run it by the editor in chief in a couple of months, after you've wowed them with your savvy and dedication." He stood, heading for the door. "I'll get you the list of things Casey was working on by tomorrow morning."

She nodded, and he was gone.

Alone in her office, Nona dropped her head, letting her forehead rest on the cool surface of her desktop. Her mother would undoubtedly be thrilled with this development, because she believed the trust of the boss was a surefire path to promotions and success. Having been in the business for ten years, Nona didn't share that belief. She saw this situation for what it was: a convenient way for the paper to get her to do more work without raising her pay. Their bottom line would improve, so why should they care about how their actions personally affected her? Her work-life balance was none of their concern.

She felt agitated, frustrated. The tumble of emotions running through her had a surprising effect, in that they made her long for Ken's steady presence. He always seemed to stay cool under pressure, and in her current state, she could use his even-keeled sensibilities.

Luckily, she would see him in a few days. Rather than burden him with her problems, she decided to hold off until Wednesday night, when they already had plans to get together.

With the bright morning sunlight illuminating the surface of his drafting table, Ken sketched in a few lines on the large sheet of paper in front of him. It was early Wednesday, and he was well into the detail stage of his sketches for the new design of the Grand Pearl. A smile lifted the corners of his mouth as he filled in the image of the rear exterior.

For Ken, this represented pure happiness. Alone in his office, with the first light of day shining on his drafting table, a pencil in his hand and a Max Roach recording playing in his headphones. His creativity was at its height, and he could feel the buzz of it flowing through his veins like electricity.

So far, he'd created twenty sketches, each illustrating a different room or view of the new theater as he envisioned it. Before he could deem his work complete, the images would be scanned into a software program to be rendered into blueprints. Once the full set of blueprints was completed, he could turn them over to the construction company that would complete the remodeling. The prospect of seeing his vision for the historic building come to life excited him. He loved the feeling just as much now as he had when he'd completed his first set of blueprints.

He got so wrapped up in detailing his sketch that he barely looked up when Lynn came into the office.

"Morning, Ken." She spoke loudly, aware of his habit of listening to music while he worked.

Hearing her over the music, he looked her way. "Morning, Lynn."

"Just letting you know I'm here if you need anything. Carry on, boss." Raising her coffee mug in his direction, she slipped out.

After she left, he directed his full attention back to putting the finishing touches on his sketch. Along the margins of the page, he neatly listed items that would be helpful to the construction foreman in carrying out his plans—dimensions, measurements, suggested building materials and finishes. He kept his pencil moving slowly, making sure that his writing would be legible. When the rendering software made the blueprints, it used text recognition to translate handwriting to typed words. Neatness was paramount in getting the desired results.

When he'd completed the page, he carefully rolled it up and placed it in an empty plastic tube. Adding the tube to the collection of the sketches he'd already drawn for the project, he went to the front of the office suite to speak briefly with Lynn.

Lynn occupied her usual seat behind the reception desk. When she heard him approaching, she looked up from her computer screen. "So how are the sketches coming for the Grand Pearl?"

"Just finished the last one." He leaned on the high partition in front of the desk, which obscured her desk and bookcase from the eyes of visitors. "We can start the rendering in a couple of days."

"So are we doing cleanup this afternoon?"

"Yes. I think it's best we get started on it." The cleanup phase was where he checked over all his drawings, erasing any elements that weren't going to be used and making sure the finished illustrations were as clean as possible so that the rendering software could read them. It wasn't the most fun, but it was a necessary part of the process.

Lynn ran a hand over her hair. "Sounds good. We'll tackle the first round after lunch."

"I'm thinking we can get it done in two days if we do about eight or ten pages today and get the rest done tomorrow."

Lynn opened her mouth, but before she could say anything, the ringing of the phone interrupted her. "Excuse me." Picking up the receiver, she answered, "Good morning, Yamada Creative. This is Lynn. How can I help you?"

Ken remained by the desk as she listened to the caller on the other end.

"Okay, sir. Let me get him for you." Lynn pressed the hold button. "It's a Nolan Cross of Crossroads Development. He says he has a project he'd like to speak to you about."

When he heard Cross's name, Ken's brow shot up. Crossroads Development handled some of the largest construction projects in the southeastern United States—everything from neighborhood schools to skyscrapers. As a result, Nolan Cross was one of the wealthiest men in the country. "I'll take it in my office."

"Got it." Lynn replaced the receiver.

He jogged down the hall and slid into his desk chair. Taking a deep breath, he picked up the handset. "Good morning, this is Ken Yamada."

"Mr. Yamada. Nolan Cross." The older man spoke in an authoritative, confident voice. "I'm CEO of Crossroads Development. How are you?"

Ken responded, keeping his tone level and professional despite the massive amount of money on the other end of the line. "Hello, Mr. Cross. I'm well aware of who you are, and I'm very well, thanks. How are you?"

"I'm well, except for one thing. I have a very large and lucrative project, and I'm in need of an architect."

"You've come to the right place," Ken quipped, keeping his tone light.

"I've been hearing a lot about your work lately. The children's hospital in Lillyville is one of the most impressive I've ever seen. My niece received care there last spring, and I was amazed at the architectural details."

"Thank you, sir." He was flattered to hear that the

prestigious Nolan Cross admired his work. "I appreciate that."

"I'm told you're restoring a historic theater there in Charlotte. The Grand Pearl. When will you wrap up that project?"

"I expect to turn over the blueprints within a week or so. By the second week of July, I'll be ready for whatever is next."

"I see. Well, let me tell you a bit about the project. Crossroads is developing a mixed-use area in Richmond, called Stone Haven. Our vision involves a mixture of condominiums and townhomes, as well as shopping and office space. We want it built with sustainable practices and materials, and we want to keep costs down enough so as not to displace the current residents. There is already enough gentrification going on in cities across the country, and Crossroads isn't interested in contributing to that."

Ken was impressed, not just with the idea, but with Nolan's commitment to the residents of the area. "This project sounds fantastic, and I really respect your efforts to do what's right for the community rather than what is most profitable."

"That's my philosophy, and it's kept this company in the black for twenty-two years." Nolan paused and drew a deep breath. "I love your vision, your drive. You've got the kind of fresh approach that I think would be great for this project. The city has pledged funds for the assignment, and along with the investors we've secured, the Stone Haven project is valued at one hundred and

fifty million dollars. The architect we choose will easily clear thirty to thirty-five million."

At that moment, Ken was glad Nolan Cross couldn't
see his expression. His eyes were probably the size of
saucers. "Wow. This really is a lucrative project."

"Now, if it were all up to me, I'd hire you right now.
But I've got a board of directors breathing down my
neck, and they're a tough bunch to convince. So we have
to hold off until the Grand Pearl project is complete."

He cringed. "I can understand that. This is a very
big project."

"So what I'll need from you is your blueprints and
sketches. Send over the ones from the Lillyville hospital, the Davenport Senior Center and the Crossley Mu-
seum, along with photos of those projects. Add the final
blueprints and sketches from the Grand Pearl project,
and I think that will give me what I need to convince
the board."

"That's not a problem. I'll have my assistant start
pulling the package together this afternoon. You'll have
everything on your desk by the end of this month."

Nolan sounded pleased. "Great. I'll look forward to
receiving it. Have a great day, Ken."

"You too, Mr. Cross."

As Ken replaced the handset, he leaned back in his
chair, releasing a pent-up breath. He couldn't believe the
turn this morning had taken. Stone Haven, if he could
clinch it, would be the largest and most profitable project he'd ever done. The amount Nolan had quoted for
the architect well surpassed the city's entire budget for
the Grand Pearl project.

Along with the flattery and gratitude he felt came a sense of unease. With a project this large, he couldn't help but feel the pressure. He'd have to knock the Grand Pearl remodel out of the park if the board at Crossroads was as hard to impress as Nolan had suggested.

He clapped his hands together, slid his chair back. If he was going to pull this off, he had no time to waste. He got up from his desk and stuck his head out the office door. "Lynn, come here, please. We've got work to do."

Chapter 10

When Nona arrived at Satori Martial Arts Wednesday evening, she knew exactly where to go. Dressed in leggings, a tank top and sneakers, she entered the building and headed straight for the corridor that led to the smaller gym area. She'd brought a workout bag with her, containing an extra set of clothes and some toiletries, in case the evening's activities made her sweaty.

She smiled as she thought about what that could mean. With the attraction crackling between her and Ken, she knew she could easily end up sweaty for reasons that had nothing to do with martial arts.

She walked into the smaller gym and found him already there. He was shirtless again, and he stood in the center of the floor, going through a series of stretches. Watching him, she mused about his attire. He'd shown her an image of the traditional Japanese kendo gear. The gear was dark and bulky and appeared very heavy. It even included a cage-like helmet worn over the head, to protect the face and eyes from any potential blows from the opponent's sword.

Yet she'd never seen Ken don the gear. Twice now she'd come here and found him topless. She was starting to wonder if he always practiced dressed that way—or if it was because he was with her.

She stood off to the side and let him finish what he was doing, but she could see him watching her in the mirror. He was aware of her presence, and she offered him a soft smile.

Finally he walked over to where she stood. He greeted her with a soft kiss on the forehead. "How was your day?"

"It was okay." She didn't really want to dwell on the stress she was facing at work, at least not now. "And yours?"

"Busy, but good."

"Can I ask you something?"

He draped an arm loosely around her waist. "I thought we were finished with the interview questions."

She giggled. "It's not that. This is just something I want to know that has nothing to do with the story."

"What is it?"

"Do you always spar with no shirt on?"

"No. I wear some modified gear when I spar. But we're not sparring. Technically, we're practicing. And I always do that without a shirt." He drew her body close to his. "Do you want me to wear a shirt?"

She felt a certain boldness awaken within her. Lifting her hand, she ran her open palm over the hard muscles of his chest and abdomen. *Swinging that bamboo sword certainly does wonders for the upper body.* "No, no. I was just curious."

A broad grin broke out over his face. "Then come on. Let's do this." He released his hold on her and walked across the floor, toward the sword rack.

She set her bag down on the floor, using her foot to slide it beneath the bench. Then she went to stand by Ken, taking the sword he extended in her direction.

"You did pretty well the last time. Like I said, I think you have a natural talent for kendo that may stem from your dance abilities." He held his sword out in front of him, with the blade pointed straight up. "I want to try something different with you, if you don't mind."

Being on a date in a martial arts studio was already well outside the norm for her, so she was game for whatever. "I'm up for it. What do you have in mind?"

He stood his sword against the wall. "I'm going to lead you through several moves, and if you do well with that, we can try a few combinations that are a bit more complex."

She nodded, widening her stance and holding her sword the way he'd held his. "Okay. Where do we start?"

"Here." He moved around her until he stood behind her.

The front of his body came into contact with the back of hers, and he draped his arms over hers, capturing her hands in his own.

A shock wave of awareness and desire moved

through her. She'd never been in such close contact with him before, and every nerve ending in her body was now alive, awake and alert to his presence.

"This way I can guide your movements more accurately." His voice was quiet, and she could feel the warmth of his breath on her neck.

Her hand trembled, and she struggled to hold on to her sword. She wanted to say something but couldn't seem to form words.

As if sensing that she was losing her grip, his hand closed around hers, effectively keeping the sword from slipping. "Tighten up, honey. We're just getting started."

She swallowed, nodded.

With slow precision, he began moving their bodies in tandem. "This is your basic stance." He spoke softly in her ears as he moved them from one position to the next, letting her know the name and purpose of each stance. By the time they moved into thrusts and swings for the sword, her heart was thumping in her ears like a drum machine.

Her breath came faster, shallower. She felt their bodies in sync, almost as if they were one, a single entity moving through space. She couldn't remember ever feeling this kind of connection with someone. It transcended the physical to touch her mentally and emotionally.

"There." He eased her hand down, letting the tip of the sword touch the floor. "How do you feel now? More confident?"

She took a minute to get herself together. It wasn't easy, since his body was still in contact with hers. "If you're talking about my confidence with the sword, then yes."

"What else would I be talking about?"

She could hear the teasing in his tone. "Don't make me throttle you, Ken."

"There was never a need to build confidence between us." He slid his right hand along her inner arm, then let his index finger glide down her side until his hand came to rest on her waist. "What's happening between us is inevitable, unavoidable and totally natural."

She trembled, and since his hand was no longer there to secure it, the sword slipped from her grip and clattered to the floor.

Paying no attention to the dropped weapon, he turned her to face him.

As their gazes connected, she could feel the hard evidence of his desire grazing her pelvis.

"Our lesson is complete, Nona. What's next?"

The sensations coursing through her body made her feel brazen, wanton. She was tired of fighting the fire between them. Ready to be consumed by it, she said, "You tell me."

"Have you ever seen a traditional Japanese garden? Because I have one behind my house that I'd love to show you." He traced his fingertips along her jawline.

She sensed that he had much more to show her than his plants. And because she wanted everything he had in store for her, she nodded. "Let's go."

Ken led Nona by the hand through his dining room, toward the sliding glass doors that led to his deck. "This way."

"Your house is really beautiful," she commented as she followed him.

"I'll show you more of it later." And he intended to do that. Right now, though, his mind was firmly set on showing her the garden and, in particular, the large, padded bench that centered it.

He unlocked the sliding door, pushing it open. A warm breeze wafted by as they stepped out onto his cedar deck. He shut the door behind them.

She walked over to the railing, taking in the wide-angle view of his garden. She said something, but he didn't hear her.

He was too busy admiring her backside. She'd worn a tank top and a pair of black leggings to the dojo. The leggings gripped every curve of her behind, leaving nothing to the imagination. While she'd probably worn them in the name of comfort, Ken couldn't help but be turned on by them.

"Wow. This is really impressive, Ken."

"Thank you." He was glad she seemed to like his backyard oasis. He'd taken great care in having his land-scaping done to very specific standards. The result was an outdoor space where he could enjoy spending his free time, and it had been well worth the effort and cost.

She pointed. "Is that a pond down there?"

He nodded. "Yes. It has a few koi in it." He tugged her hand gently. "Come on down the stairs and you can see it up close."

They walked down the flight of stairs that led them down to the yard. There, he slowed his footsteps, point-ing out things to her as they moved through the yard.

"There are ten Japanese maples planted back here. Around the perimeter are pine trees, which symbolize longevity. I also have some clumping bamboo, azalea bushes and some water iris in the pond."

She nodded, taking in the sights as they walked along. "It's even more beautiful close up. I'm glad you brought me here."

They neared his solid oak bench. It was situated beneath a Japanese maple and in the perfect spot to view the koi swimming around in the pond. He took a seat on the cushion. Patting the seat next to him, he beckoned her to join him. When she did, he draped an arm around her shoulders. As much as he wanted her, he didn't want her to feel rushed or pressured in any way. So, until she let him know she was ready, he'd be content to sit here with her in the silence, holding her close.

She continued to look around the garden as she spoke. "Do you have any neighbors close by?"

He thought the question was a bit odd, but he shook his head. "No. The lots in this neighborhood range between one and a half and three acres. There isn't another house near mine, at least not for a few miles."

Turning his way, she met his eyes. "Then you can make love to me out here, and no one would be able to hear us."

His brow hitched in surprise. While he'd wanted her to see the garden, he hadn't expected her to boldly ask him to make love to her here. "I suppose that's true."

She eased closer to him, wrapping her arms around his waist. "Kiss me."

So he did, letting his lips crush hers. Soon their

tongues were mating and dancing, and he gathered her closer to him so that he could experience every drop of passion she had to give.

The kiss ended, and when he pulled back, he could see how breathless she looked. "Are you sure you want to…out here?"

She nodded, reaching for him. "Yes."

Eager to grant her wish, he began stroking her arms. When she lifted them, he dragged the tank up and over her head, then draped it over the back of the bench. She wore a bra that hooked in the front, much to his delight. With his gaze locked with hers, he slowly undid the clasps running down the center of the garment, then spread the open halves.

Lowering his head, he placed soft kisses on the swell of her breasts before moving on to capture a dark nipple in his mouth. He heard her sharp intake of breath in response to his actions, and he reveled in her enjoyment. He lingered there for as long as he felt necessary, and when he'd thoroughly pleased one nipple, he moved on to the other. By the time he drew away, she'd slumped against the bench's backrest, her breaths rapid and shallow.

He wanted her out of her clothes but knew she probably couldn't stand in her current state. Leaning back, he took in the erotic sight she made, lying on his bench with her bra open. Her breasts were exposed to his eyes and the moonlight. Slowly, he raised her hips and began to tug down her leggings, until he revealed the full length of her long, bronze legs. The leggings joined her tank draped over the back of the bench. Her eyes remained closed.

He'd never been so grateful for the privacy his home afforded, and he planned to take full advantage of it.

He stood and then knelt in front of the bench. It took her a moment to realize what he was about to do, but when he grasped her ankles and gently lifted until the soles of her feet rested on the edge of the bench, she suddenly snapped back to awareness.

She murmured, "Ken, I…"

"Shh." He could not resist the lure of her. Would she taste as sweet as he imagined? He knew of only one way to find out. He tapped her inner thighs gently and watched as they fell open. Only a thin strip of black lace stood between him and what he imagined would be the sweetest dessert a man could ever enjoy. He used gentle fingertips to push the lace aside, the fragrance of her arousal enticing him, spurring him on. The last thing he saw before he leaned in was the unmistakable trembling of anticipation that had taken over her thighs.

His tongue worked over her warm flesh, and she dissolved into soft, whimpering cries. Nothing on earth would have prepared him for her sweetness or her responsiveness. The more she writhed beneath him, the more she cried out, the more he wanted of her. She was a woman made for pleasure, a goddess possessing carnal powers so potent, he couldn't help falling under her spell. His manhood pulsed, craving the feel of her body surrounding his. He held it at bay, because he wanted to take her to the heights with his mouth first.

Soon her cries climbed an octave, then another, until

she shattered with a strangled scream. Only then, when he was sure she'd been properly prepared, did he pull away from her sweet, honeyed treasure.

Getting to his feet again was complicated by the throbbing hardness in his trousers, but he managed. He gently rid her of the panties, added them to the pile of her clothes. When he took her, he wanted her nude in his arms so he could store the memory of her body in his mind forever. He wanted to be able to recall every bronze inch of her.

"Nona." He called her name.

She opened her eyes. "Hmm?" Her tone conveyed the ecstasy she'd just experienced.

"We need to move this to my bedroom. This bench isn't big enough for everything I have in store for you." And it wasn't. In order to make love to her in the way she deserved, he would need the comfort and space afforded by the king-size bed in his master suite.

She lifted her arms to him.

He gathered her up as she pressed the wad of her discarded clothing to her chest. With her over his shoulder, he swatted her behind as he began the walk back up to the house.

She purred, and he knew it was going to be one hell of a night.

Chapter 11

Nona sighed as Ken laid her atop his bed. It was huge, king-size, she assumed, and covered with the most wonderfully soft comforter that felt like satin against her skin. She couldn't tell if the bed was really as comfortable as it seemed, or if she just felt that way because of Ken.

He turned on a lamp. "Make yourself comfortable, honey."

She smiled, loving the way he referred to her as "honey." No man had ever called her that before. Men had called her "baby," "shorty" and a few other ridiculous nicknames, and usually she hated it. But something about the way Ken said it made it so appealing.

As she stretched out on the bed, he remained on his feet. She watched him undress, anticipating everything they would soon share. He'd already given her so much ecstasy, she couldn't wait to see what else he had in store for her.

After he'd stripped off his tee and sweatpants, he moved to his dresser and opened one of the top drawers. He reappeared next to the bed, and she could see him in the circle of light cast by his lamp. He wore a pair of black bikini briefs, and as her eyes fell on them, she could clearly see the hardness outlined there. She licked her lips. While she observed him, he hooked his fingers in the waistband of the garment and dragged it down. At her first look at him, she inhaled deeply and sucked her teeth. "Damn."

He smiled. "So you like what you see?"

Oh, hell, yes. She nodded, mesmerized by the sight of him rolling on the condom. She couldn't tear her eyes away from him, nor could she think of anything else.

He began moving toward her, and she crawled to the center of the bed. By the time he climbed in with her, she was on her back with her thighs parted in invitation.

He kissed her on the lips. "Ready?"

He'd made sure of that outside under the stars. "Yes, baby."

He crushed his lips to hers while his big hands stroked their way from her shoulders to her hips. Once he was there, he put a firm but gentle grip on her ass. Lifting her, he thrust his pelvis forward to meet hers.

She uttered an unladylike curse at the sensation of him entering her, filling her. Her body stretched around him, adjusting to him, welcoming him. He pulled back only to thrust forward again, and she moaned low in her throat. Still gripping her, he settled into a slow and steady rhythm, giving her all of him, then easing away only to plunge inside her again. Grabbing hold of his strong shoulders, she held on tight as her body rose to meet his.

Sparks ignited between her thighs, rising from the magical friction of his body moving within her. She could hear the sounds she made, though she had no control over them. Since she'd never known pleasure like this, her own voice sounded foreign. But as the sensations rose and built, pushing her closer and closer to another climax, she moaned louder, not caring how she sounded or who might hear. The only things in the world that mattered to her were him, his big hands holding her hips and his glorious hardness moving between her thighs.

He growled, lifting her hips higher and picking up the pace of his thrusts. She could tell he was getting close, and so was she. She clung to him, her hands beginning to slip as beads of perspiration gathered on his shoulders. The comforter beneath them slid back and forth, rustling in time with his thrusts.

Her body tingled all over, radiating from her core. The building pleasure finally became too much, and as she clawed at his back and shoulders, she came for the second time, her body pulsing around his.

Moments later, he roared as he reached his own completion. As it subsided, he slowed his thrusts, then stopped. Releasing his grip on her hips, he let his manhood slip out of her and rolled over to lie next to her.

She lay in the dim light, trying to catch her breath

and regain control of her mind. She could hear his heavy breathing as he lay next to her, and she realized that he'd just treated her to the best lovemaking she'd ever experienced.

He shifted, draped his arms over her stomach. She snuggled closer to him, loving how safe she felt nestled next to him this way.

Neither of them spoke, because words were unnecessary. The connection that had been growing between them since the day they first met had now been solidified. She knew it, and she sensed that he knew it as well. She tried not to overthink what was happening, because she didn't want anything to infringe on the sensual joy of this moment.

She thought of rolling over to talk to him, but before she could change positions, she heard his soft snores ruffling the silence. Smiling, she closed her own eyes and let the exhaustion brought on by his lovemaking take hold.

Darkness still filled the room when Ken opened his eyes. He shifted around in the bed a bit, seeking Nona's warm nudity. It took a few moments for him to shake off the grogginess, and when he did, he realized she wasn't in the bed with him.

Sitting up, he let his eyes scan the shadows of the room while he listened for signs of her presence. Nothing about Nona made him think she'd creep out of bed and leave in the middle of the night after lovemaking, so he assumed she was still in the house somewhere.

He heard the sound of water running, and then her

quiet footsteps. A moment later, she returned to the bedroom. He flipped on the bedside lamp, and as the soft light illuminated the room, he could see that she'd put on the black-and-gold kimono his father had given him for his twenty-fifth birthday.

"I found this in your closet. I hope you don't mind me wearing it."

"It's fine. You look better in it than I do." Seeing her body wrapped in the expensive, handmade silk garment made him smile. The way the fabric draped over her ample curves made the blood rush to his manhood all over again.

She giggled, shaking her head as she brought her glass of water over to the bed. Setting it down on the nightstand, she took a seat on the edge of the bed. "You didn't think I snuck out, did you? I was thirsty, and I think you know why."

"I do." From his position lying on his side, he sat up and put his back against the headboard.

She moved to sit in between his thighs, resting her back against him. A soft sigh escaped her. "I feel so comfortable with you. Like I've known you forever."

"Good." He draped his arms around her, holding her warmth close to him. Her hair smelled of some sweet, floral shampoo, and he inhaled the scent.

"You know, you're one of the few people in my life to tell me that my dance skills are useful."

He didn't know where that had come from, but he liked that she felt she could talk to him. "Oh?"

"My friends don't really take it seriously, and neither do my parents. My mom especially. She's always trying to convince me to quit teaching. But I love dance, and I love my students. She just doesn't get it."

"It would be a shame for someone with moves like you to stop dancing." He emphasized his comment with a small pelvic thrust.

A peal of laughter escaped her. "Quit it, Ken."

He smiled, even though he knew she couldn't see it. "Seriously, though. Remember what I said about not doing anything that doesn't spark passion within?"

She nodded. "Yeah, I remember."

"I already know dance is something you have passion for. Do you have passion for journalism?" He genuinely wanted to know the answer.

She was quiet for a moment, as if thinking about it. "You know what? It used to excite me, but it doesn't anymore. There have been so many changes in the industry that now it just feels stressful most of the time."

"Hmm." He didn't want to tell her how she should live her life—they were both adults. But he hoped she could see what he'd just pointed out.

"Crap." She turned her head, looked into his eyes. "I'm burned out on reporting, aren't I? I should be teaching dance full-time."

He shrugged. "That's your decision to make, not your parents' or anyone else's."

She gifted him with a sweet smile. "Thank you, Ken."

"No problem." He watched her as she turned back around, then snuggled down into his embrace again. They lay in silence for a few moments, with only the sounds of their breathing to fill the room. He thought about what she'd just revealed to him and how he'd been so guarded with her. Now that they'd made love, he felt that the last barrier between them had fallen. She'd shared her body and soul with him, and it didn't seem right to go on hiding things from her.

She seemed to sense his thoughts, because she asked, "What is it?"

"I feel like… I can trust you with my family's story. But this has to be strictly off the record. It can't make it into your article under any circumstances."

She sat up, turned her body in his arms. "I would never betray your trust, Ken. Besides, I've already turned in my draft article."

Looking into her eyes made it easy to believe her. Giving her a squeeze, he began. "When my mother was in that car accident, she was carrying a child."

Nona's hand went to cover her mouth. "Oh, my God. There was no mention of that in anything I read. I'm so sorry."

"My father purposefully hid my mother's pregnancy from the public. He was still a trusted adviser to the commissioner at the time. Though he'd left the position, he was still in the public eye. You should know that the baby was delivered before my mother's death, and that the child survived."

Her eyes grew wide. "So you're not an only child?"

He shook his head. "I have a sister, Miyu. She's just turned twenty-one. No one in my life knows about her, not Lynn, not my bandmates."

Her brow furrowed. "I don't understand. Why was

your father so determined to hide your sister's existence? And why were you?"

He drew a deep breath, released it. "Because Miyu is not my father's child."

Nona tensed. "Oh."

"My mother had an affair during the last year of her life. Miyu is the result of that affair. Rather than suffer the embarrassment of having people know that my mother was unfaithful, my father made sure to keep Miyu's birth a secret."

"I'm still confused. Why not raise her as his own, without telling anyone she was fathered by another man?"

"Two reasons. One is resentment. My father wasn't terribly interested in raising another man's child. The other was practical. Miyu isn't fully Japanese. Her father was black, so…" He didn't finish the sentence because he knew he didn't have to.

She blinked several times, her face conveying surprise and amazement. "Wow. This is a pretty wild story, but it does explain a lot. Now I understand why you are so private."

He nodded. "I raised Miyu. She's fifteen years younger than me, and my father was very distant with her. Miyu lived with us in my father's home, but that was about as much as he was willing to do for her. When I left home at eighteen, I took Miyu with me. With the help of our housekeeper, Frances, I made sure Miyu had everything she needed until she went off to college. I love her, Nona. Even though my father never grew to love her, she is my sister, and the last link to my mother."

She brought her hand up to stroke his jaw. "I understand, and I admire you for taking on the responsibility of another person when you were still a kid yourself."

Her praise brought the smile back to his face. "Thank you. I'm sure your boss at the paper would salivate over a scoop like this. But my father is old and not in the best health. I'm not sure he could handle it if this were to get out."

"I promise, this won't go any further than me." She tilted her head, pressing her lips against his.

When the kiss ended, he slid down in bed, taking her with him until he was lying on his back with her straddling his waist.

She opened the kimono, a wicked smile lighting her face.

He reached over and flicked off the lamp, plunging the room back into darkness.

Chapter 12

"I'm telling you, he's amazing." Nona spoke into the receiver so that Hadley could hear her. The cell phone reception around her house was dicey at best.

Sheba, curled up on the floor by the sofa, snorted in her sleep as she shifted positions.

"I believe you, Nona. You don't have to shout." Hadley laughed on the tail of her statement.

"Sorry. You know how the reception is in my house." Holding the phone to her ear with one hand, she held a glass of iced tea in the other hand. In her bunny slippers, she padded to the couch, stepped over the dog and settled in for an evening with her favorite Thursday night television shows. In order to get more comfortable, she pushed aside her still-open briefcase, filled with her papers from work.

"I can't believe you slept with him already. It's only been two weeks."

"Whatever. The loving was so good, I took a sick day from work today."

"Damn, girl. You needed recovery time? It's like that?"

"Hell, yeah!"

"You are such a mess, Nona."

Nona scoffed. "Hadley, have you forgotten who you're talking to? I remember all the wild mess you pulled in your early twenties. Who was that guy you took home on your twenty-second birthday? The one with the fro-hawk and the leather pants?"

Hadley quieted for a moment before she answered. "Oh. You mean Snake."

"Snake? Come on, girl. You never found out his real name?"

"Listen, the way he lived up to that nickname, I didn't care about his real name." She laughed aloud.

Shaking her head, Nona turned on her forty-inch flat-screen television. "See what I mean? You are in no place to judge me, missy."

"I guess you're right. I'll stop teasing you, because I want all the juicy details of your encounter with your drummer–slash–architect–slash–master athlete." The sound of Hadley's gum chewing filled the line.

"I'm not telling you anything until you quit popping that damn gum in my ear, girl." She waited.

The sound stopped, then Hadley spoke again. "All right, *Mom*." Hadley always called Nona that when she thought she was being bossy. "So, what was it like being with a…you know…?"

"A Japanese guy?" Nona completed the sentence for her.

"Well, yeah. I mean I'm not one to stereotype or anything but, I mean, what was *it* like?"

Nona settled into the cushions of her sofa, tucking her feet beneath her. "To be perfectly honest, it wasn't that different from any other guy I've been with."

"Lies you tell. The way you were giggling when you first called me, I know this man is working with something spectacular." Hadley's tone conveyed her absolute surety that she was right.

Rolling her eyes, Nona acquiesced. "I'm not about to tell you all his business. But what he was working with was more than enough to satisfy me."

"Ooh!" Hadley squealed in her ear. "Girl, tell me more!"

"No. I'm not telling you anything else, nosy."

"You're no fun." Hadley pouted, as she often did when she was denied gossip.

Nona didn't care. She was still in the throes of bliss from what she'd shared with Ken. It was special and something she wanted to keep to herself. Hadley would get over it.

"Whatever. Anyway, did I tell you about Marques?"

Nona's brow crinkled as she flipped the channels on her television. "The guy you met when we were in Vegas last year? What about him?"

"Girl, he called me a couple of days ago. I was at the office, sitting at my desk. Savion and Campbell had gone out to lunch, but Savion came back while I was on the phone."

"Oh, Lord." She knew something crazy was coming as soon as Hadley mentioned her brothers.

"Do you know that fool snatched my phone, yelled at Marques, then hung up on him? It was a hot mess."

"How did he even know who you were talking to?"

"He didn't. He said I was smiling so hard it must have been 'some dude.' I'm telling you, they want me to be single until I die."

"Did you get him back?"

"Sure did. Popped him right upside the back of his square head. I love my brother, but he gets on my last nerve sometimes."

Nona couldn't hold back her laugh. Having been around Hadley as long as she had, she was quite familiar with the overprotective antics of her older brothers. "They're going to come around one day, I promise."

"Hopefully that day will come before my ovaries shut down production." She groaned. "Look, let me get off the phone. Mama is calling me. Later, girl."

"'Bye, Hadley." She disconnected the call and lent her full focus to the television.

About twenty minutes into her show, she frowned. She'd missed a few episodes, and now she had no clue what was going on. She could tell something about the show's dynamic had changed, and one of her favorite characters was inexplicably missing from the episode. Annoyed, she turned off the TV and got up, careful not to step on her still slumbering pup.

A few minutes later, she was back on the couch with

her journal and a pen. She realized that in the digital age, journaling on paper would probably be considered old-fashioned. Regardless, she enjoyed the feeling of peace she got from venting on paper. No one even knew she kept a journal, so it was the perfect place for her to record her innermost thoughts and feelings. There were some things she didn't even want to tell Hadley but still wanted to work through. Those were the things that went into the pages of her journal.

With her pen in hand, she jotted down her memories of the previous night. Staying over at Ken's house hadn't been her intention, but the passions brewing between them had finally boiled over at the gym. Now that she'd given herself to him, she felt the shift in their relationship. So far, she had no regrets. They'd shared a night filled with ecstasy, and she knew she would never forget it. He'd awakened something in her, something that had been lying dormant for years.

Her pursuit of her career at the newspaper had left her very little time for dating. She'd seen a few men over the past decade, but not that many. She'd only reached the physical stage of the relationship with two of them. And until now, it always seemed that once she'd slept with a guy, her attraction to him started to fizzle.

With Ken, things were very different. Now that she'd been with him, all she could think about was when she'd get the chance to make love to him again. He'd been gentle and considerate, yet strong and powerful when she'd needed him to be. Her body tingled at the thought of his caressing hands and the kisses he'd placed over every inch of her skin.

She also wrote down the story he'd told her about his family, because she was still processing that. The tale he'd told was a lot to take in. He'd been right when he described how excited Huff would be to know the sordid details of the Yamada family's past. But she'd promised not to reveal his business, and she intended to keep her word. He'd trusted her with something he'd never told anyone else, not even his bandmates, whom he considered his closest friends. To honor the trust he'd placed in her, she knew she had to protect his secrets.

She stifled a yawn as she continued to jot down her thoughts. What he'd said about her teaching dance, and his advice to follow her passion, still echoed in her mind. Working at the paper just wasn't the same as when she'd first started. Her mother would freak out if she knew her daughter was even entertaining the idea of teaching dance full-time. Nona wondered if she would ever have the courage to walk away from the job she no longer loved in favor of the one that filled her soul with joy.

Sheba's scratching at the door got her attention. Realizing the dog needed to go out, she closed her journal and tossed it onto the couch. "Okay, girl. I'll let you out."

As she walked away to open the door for the dog, she didn't look back to see where her journal landed.

Ken walked into the kitchen, headed for the sink to wash his hands.

His sister, Miyu, stood nearby, chopping green onions atop a silicone cutting board.

As he shook his hands dry before grabbing a paper towel, some of the droplets hit his sister.

Miyu rolled her eyes. "Can you not throw water all over my kitchen, please?"

Ken wiped his hands, then tossed the paper towel into the trash can. "Stop being so dramatic, Miyu."

"Keep it up and I'm not having you over for dinner anymore."

"I'm your big brother, and you can't get rid of me." He leaned down and kissed her on the cheek.

She smiled. "Just help me get this stir-fry ready, would you?"

He decided to stop teasing her for the moment. His growling stomach reminded him that he'd never get to eat if they didn't finish cooking.

The two of them worked in convivial silence to put the finishing touches on the teriyaki stir-fry they were making. The galley kitchen in Miyu's apartment wasn't terribly spacious, especially compared to the one in his house. But getting around the space was easy since his sister was so compact.

Ken stood almost a foot taller than Miyu. At twenty-one, she was the same height she'd been since the age of sixteen: five feet, four inches. She was petite, and she'd let her wavy black hair grow so long that it almost overpowered her tiny body. It reached her lower back when it was down, but at the moment she had it piled on top of her head in a messy ponytail. Crystals of the brown sugar she'd used to make the homemade teriyaki sauce clung to her hands. The sugar was only a shade darker than her rich olive skin. He stopped stirring the vegetables and shrimp to watch her as she stood on a step stool to pull down dishes from her upper cabinets. Even with the step stool beneath her, she still had to stretch to reach the plates. He chuckled, because he knew it was pure stubbornness that kept her from asking him to get the plates down for her.

Eventually, she sensed him watching her. Turning her big brown eyes in his direction, she said, "What?"

"Nothing." He went back to stirring the food.

"Ken, why were you staring at me?" She set the plates on the counter as she climbed down from the step stool. "And if you give me some goofy speech about how much I've grown, I swear I'll give you such a smack."

He looked down at her. "Where? You can't reach me from down there."

"Maybe not, but I can give you a pretty good kick in the shins from down here." She pursed her lips, lifting her foot as if she intended to let him have it right then.

He abandoned his wooden spoon, leaving it in the wok as he darted away, moving out of his sister's reach.

Laughing, she moved to the stove and took over the stirring. Lowering the heat, she jerked her head toward the dining table. "It's almost ready. Set the table, goofball."

He gathered the plates and silverware she'd left on the counter and took them to her small table. Once he'd set them up, he returned to the kitchen to get the pitcher of chilled green tea from the refrigerator.

A few minutes later, they were seated at the table, enjoying the stir-fry and each other's company.

"So, how are things in the exciting world of pharmaceuticals?" Ken forked up a helping of shrimp, vegetables and rice as he waited for Miyu's answer.

"Great. You know I love my work, and as much as you tease me about being a nerd, we both know I'm doing something vitally important." She was a recent graduate, having received her bachelor's degree in chemical engineering from North Carolina State University the previous month. Due to an internship during her senior year, she was already working in an entry-level position for a Charlotte-based medical company, NuVeda. The company made several types of medicine but specialized in chemotherapy drugs. "Fridays are usually pretty crazy in the office, but hey, we're saving lives."

"No argument from me. Your work is definitely important, and you know I'm proud of you."

She smiled. "Thanks. By the way, how's Hiro?"

"He's doing okay. I'm trying to get him to rest more, but you know how stubborn he is." While Miyu always referred to Ken's father by his first name, she still cared enough about him to ask after him whenever she and Ken saw each other, and Ken appreciated that.

"I wonder if he knows we have that in common." She made the comment between bites of stir-fry.

Before he could say anything in response, Miyu's phone pinged in her pocket.

He watched her take the phone out and look at the screen. She read something there, and her smile broadened. Her cheeks flushed slightly as she tucked the phone back in her pocket.

His brow hitched. "What was that about?"

"None of your business, goofball."

He gave her his sternest look. "Miyu."

She rolled her eyes. "His name is Kevin. We had a couple of classes together these past couple of school years."

"And?"

"And, what?" Miyu took a drink from her glass of tea.

Folding his arms over his chest, he waited.

"Ugh." She rested her forehead in her hand. "We've been talking for a while and he wants to take me out to a movie. Is that okay with you, Warden?"

He shrugged, since he didn't really know much about this Kevin character who'd been making eyes at his baby sister. "I don't know. Where does he live? What does he do for a living? Who does he—"

"Lay off." She cut him off before he finished his last question. "I know what I need to know about him. And since he asked me to the movies and not to get married, I'm not going to entertain your questions."

Ken frowned but backed off. He knew Miyu was stubborn, always had been. If he kept pressing her, she would lay her most epic silent treatment on him. It was either back off now or have his sister block his calls and avoid all contact with him for weeks on end.

"Kenny, you know I love you, and I appreciate everything you've done for me." Miyu reached across the table to squeeze his hand. "But regardless of all that, you're my brother, not my dad. You've got to let me live my life."

He sighed. "Sorry, Miyu. You know I can't help myself sometimes. When I heard you talking about that guy, the old protective instincts kicked in."

She crinkled her nose at him.

"But that's no excuse. I'm really proud of what you've accomplished, and I respect you as an adult. So if you like this guy, and you want to go out with him, go ahead, and have fun."

A bright smile lit up her face. "Thanks, Kenny."

"But not too much fun." Jokingly, he shook a finger at her.

She responded with a playful punch to his shoulder. "Goofball."

"Whatever. You know you love me." Laughing, he scooped up another forkful of food.

Chapter 13

"Okay, class. Let's move into second position, arms and legs, please." Nona modeled the position for her students, giving them time to reproduce her positioning.

As usual, she moved between the rows of students to reposition those who were a bit off. Once everyone was in the correct position, she went to the corner of the room where she kept her boom box, atop a small table.

"I'm going to start the music. Let's run through the recital routine once, so I can see how much of it you've committed to memory." After a brief countdown, she started the compact disc that had the dance music on it.

As the music filled the room, she clapped along to help the kids keep time. Her eyes swept over them as she circled the group, assessing them as they moved. She could see that most of them had mastered the opening few steps and turns but began to falter as the song moved into its first chorus. Still, she let the song play to the end, letting the kids complete the routine to the best of their ability. Once the music ended and the kids returned to their resting stance, she returned to the front of the room.

"Your opening moves are looking very good, class. We'll need to practice the rest of the routine more, but I think you're all off to a very good start."

Betty began shifting her weight from side to side, then giggled.

Nona looked her way, knowing something had her distracted. "What's so funny, Betty?"

In response, the young girl pointed behind her. "There's a man in the door, Ms. Nona."

Turning around toward the entrance to the classroom, Nona smiled when she saw Ken standing in the doorway. In his arms he carried a huge bouquet of sunny yellow roses.

Turning back to her students, Nona spoke. "Class, can you all sit down for me for a moment? I'll be right back." She waited for the children to comply with her request, then strolled over to the door.

"Hi." He wore a Cheshire cat grin on his handsome face.

"What are you doing here?"

"I came to give you these." He extended the flowers in her direction. "And this." He gave her a peck on the cheek.

A few giggles erupted from the little girls in the class.

Blushing, she took the flowers. "Thank you. I'll take these into the break room and put them in some water." She eased around his muscular frame with the blooms.

When she returned, he'd entered the classroom fully, and the students were peppering him with questions. The queries were flying like buckshot on a quail hunt, but he didn't seem flustered or uncomfortable in the least.

"Are you Ms. Nona's friend?" Marie asked.

"Yes, I am," Ken answered easily.

"Where are you from?" Ralph fixed curious eyes on Ken.

"I was born and raised here in Charlotte, but my family is from Japan, if that's what you mean." Ken looked toward the young boy who'd posed the question.

"Ooh! Say something in Japanese!" Diamond, who could barely contain her excitement, asked.

"Aete ureshī yo."

"That was so cool!" Diamond's brow crinkled in confusion. "But…what does it mean?"

Ken laughed. "It means 'pleased to meet you.'"

Nona could feel the smile stretching across her face. Hearing Ken speak Japanese did something to her, something she couldn't dwell on while they were in a room full of children.

"Are you Ms. Nona's honey bear? My mommy calls my daddy her honey bear," Betty commented.

Instead of fielding that question, Ken swung his gaze to her. "I'm not sure. Ms. Nona, *am* I your honey bear?" His tone was playful.

Nona couldn't hold back her laugh. Her students

could always be counted on to keep things interesting. Meeting his eyes, she gave her response. "I wasn't sure, but the flowers put you over the top. So, yes, you are my honey bear."

Girlish giggles erupted from the female students, but the boys were either wearing confused looks or making gagging noises.

With a shake of her head, Nona looked at the wall clock. "Looks like that was our class chat for tonight. You all can go ahead and get ready for pickup time."

As the children got up from their seats on the floor and began bouncing around the space, Nona extended her hand toward Ken. "You are really something else."

"Your students are very bright. Inquisitive, too." He captured her hand in his own, raising it to his lips to kiss it. "You've got a great group here."

"Thanks again for the flowers. They're beautiful."

"Beautiful blooms for my beautiful blossom." He grazed slow, gentle fingertips over her jawline.

She let her eyes communicate the desire she felt building inside her. "Listen. I've got to make sure the kids get home safely. But I promise to thank you properly for your gift and your visit soon enough."

"I can't wait." He gave her a peck on the cheek and began moving away.

She let her fingertips remain connected to his as long as possible, stretching her arm as he walked out the door. After he left, she stood there for a few seconds, wearing a goofy smile. Inside, she felt like an adolescent girl in the throes of a major crush.

Diamond sidled up beside her, grinning. "You've got it pretty bad, don't you, Ms. Nona?"

She nodded. "Yeah, looks like I do."

"I like him. He's nice." With a wave, Diamond went to the main entrance of the dance school. "See you later, Ms. Nona."

"'Bye, Diamond." As if Ken hadn't already won her over, he'd now endeared himself to her students. He'd already shown himself to be a gentleman, a talented artist, athletic and a considerate lover. *Can he really be this great? What's the catch?*

Though the skeptic in her told her that Ken was too good to be true, the romantic in her didn't want to believe that. She just wanted to keep seeing him and find out where things went.

The band rehearsed on Saturday morning, then headed over to their favorite spot for lunch. By a quarter after noon they had their usual booth at the Brash Bull and were waiting for their order of forty buffalo wings with veggies and dip to arrive.

Ken stifled a yawn as his eyes darted between the televisions blaring various sports. He never really paid much attention to any of it, except when the summer Olympics rolled around. Then he watched all the track and field events with rapt interest. The rest of his bandmates had a long-standing love of football, but personally, he could take it or leave it.

Marco, who'd been uncharacteristically quiet during rehearsal, finally spoke. "Guys, I've got something to show you. It was in my mailbox yesterday." He reached into his pocket and pulled out a small, oblong box. It was see-through, and as he set it in the center of the table, everyone leaned in to study it. Inside the box was an aged piece of black fabric.

Ken was the first to ask the question on everyone's mind. "What is it?"

"It's one of Coltrane's personal saxophone straps, according to the label on the bottom." He flipped the box so everyone could read the words there.

"Holy crap. That's amazing!" Rashad reached out for the box.

Marco blocked his hand. "No way. Look, but don't touch. This is a piece of music history."

Darius shook his head in disbelief. "Let me guess. There was a note from the Music Man with the box, right?"

Marco nodded, chuckling. "Yes. Whoever this guy is, he's got some serious connections." Tucking the box back into his pocket, he settled into the leather seat. "This baby is going in a place of honor in my house."

"He's left us all something at this point. An item of great significance that's somehow attached to our jazz icons." Rashad laced his fingers together.

"Everyone except me." Ken felt a little left out at this point, but he assumed his gift from the Music Man would be forthcoming. "But I noticed he sent you guys something only after you were in a committed relationship with a woman. Maybe that has something to do with it."

Darius scratched his chin. "Good point, Ken. I mean, whoever he is, he knows enough about our lives to know when we've settled down. If he wasn't leaving us these priceless gifts, I'd be concerned he was some weird stalker."

"He never makes contact with us until he leaves a package, so I'd say he's probably not the homicidal type." Rashad shrugged. "I had Monk's sheet music professionally framed. It's hanging in my living room."

"I did the same thing with the Duke's signed photo," Darius commented.

The waitress appeared then, setting their order in the center of the table. After she'd distributed the plates and napkins, she left to take care of other tables.

While they dug into the wings, Marco asked, "What's going on with you and your reporter, Ken? Is she still pumping you for information?"

He shook his head as he spooned ranch dressing onto his plate. "Nah. She says she has everything she needs for the article, so thankfully, the interviews are done."

"So she's finally out of your hair," Rashad quipped.

He hesitated for a moment before admitting the truth. "Not exactly. We're sort of seeing each other."

"What do you mean, sort of?" Darius asked between mouthfuls. "Either you're seeing her or you ain't."

He said nothing, choosing instead to stuff a piece of celery into his mouth.

Marco slapped him on the back. "You are seeing her! Ken's finally got a woman."

"If only the Brash Bull served champagne!" Rashad laughed.

Rolling his eyes, Ken swallowed the celery. "Yes,

I'm seeing Nona. She's amazing, I enjoy her company and she's great with kids."

Everyone at the table paused. No one chewed, drank or spoke, and all eyes were suddenly on Ken.

"What?"

"Good with kids? How do you know that?" Darius asked.

"She teaches a dance class. Jazz dance. I went over there to take her flowers and—"

"Yo! Hold on, player. You bought her flowers?" Rashad's face had morphed into a mask of wide-eyed disbelief. "The same dude who vowed that no woman would ever get under his skin or distract him from his life is taking a woman flowers?"

Marco was shaking his head slowly. "I can't believe it. This woman must have magic and sunshine under her dress."

"Well, she does, but that's not why I—"

Rashad gasped loudly, clutching his chest and acting as if he were going to fall out of the booth. "Dude, so you already hit it, then? Marco's right. She put a spell on you."

"I can't believe Ken the Zen got taken down like that, man." Darius chuckled as he took a drink from his bottled beer. "This is a day that's going down in history, for real."

"I don't know about y'all, but I'm buying a lottery ticket as soon as I leave here today."

Grabbing a carrot stick, Ken tossed it at Rashad's head. "You're an idiot, you know that?"

Plucking the carrot stick from his hair, Rashad tossed

it aside. "Whatever, man." He stuck out his hand. "Welcome to the ranks. Nice to have you join us, finally."

Shaking his head, Ken shook hands with each of his friends. He realized their reactions were warranted. For the longest time, he'd been in denial that any woman could affect him. Aside from that, he'd teased them as they became enamored with the women in their lives. Now that it was happening to him, they deserved to have their fun. He smiled, because their jokes didn't bother him in the least. Having Nona in his life was worth any amount of foolishness they could dish out.

By way of changing the subject, Ken asked, "Darius, how's the family?"

A proud smile came over Darius's face. "Thanks for asking, man. JoJo is five and half months old now, and he's trying to sit up on his own. I think Eve is adjusting pretty well to being home with him, considering how hard she worked at FTI. She's great with him."

"That's good to hear, man." Marco reached out to bump fists with Darius. "I'm going to need some pointers from you when Joi delivers. She's only about seven weeks along now, and I'm already nervous as hell."

"You know I'm here for you, man. When it comes to raising a family with the woman you love, the old saying applies." Darius held up his open palms. "Ain't nothing to it but to do it."

Rashad swiped a napkin over his mouth. "We're still searching for the right child to adopt. Lina and I don't have any desire to go through the baby stage, so we're looking to take in an older child."

Listening to his friends talk about their families

made Ken smile. He enjoyed seeing them so happy. It also made him think about his future. Would Nona be his wife? Would she one day give him beautiful little curly-haired babies? Things were so new now, he had no way of knowing. Whatever their future together looked like, he was glad to be along for the ride.

"You got quiet, Ken." Marco ribbed him.

"Just…thinking about the future." Since his boys knew Nona had hooked him, he saw no need to try to hide it.

"I'll bet." Darius chuckled. "Just let things happen naturally. You're gonna get there one day."

As he took a drink of root beer, Ken wondered just how long he'd have to wait.

Chapter 14

Dragging herself to the break room for her third cup of coffee, Nona stifled a yawn. It was around two o'clock on a Wednesday afternoon, the point at which it seemed the workweek would never come to an end. After an entire morning spent rewriting her feature article and eating lunch at her desk while she proofed one of Crystal's articles, she was running on empty.

Once she'd fixed the coffee to her liking, she trudged back to her office and plopped down in her desk chair. What she wanted more than anything was to take a nap. Eyeing the stacks of paper on her desk, she seriously considered knocking everything off the desktop and resting her forehead there so she could catch a few quick minutes of sleep. Knowing that was impossible, she took a long draw from her coffee mug instead.

Porter, the department intern, rapped on her office door. "Excuse me. Can I come in, Ms. Gregory?" The ever chipper Porter was in his junior year as a dual journalism and English major at UNC Charlotte. He was the only intern at the paper who kept working through the summer; while his peers went home for vacation, he stayed and took summer classes. His short blond hair was styled with gel into some sort of spiky do, and his blue eyes always seemed to hold a hint of humor, as if he was in on a joke no one else knew about.

"Come on in, Porter." She waved him into the room. "What do you need?"

"Mr. Huffman asked me to see if you're done with the second draft of your feature." He stood on the other side of her desk, careful not to infringe on her personal space.

She shook her head. Despite the hours she'd spent on the article already, she wasn't satisfied with it. "Not yet. Tell him I'll have it ready by five."

"Sure thing. I'll come back and pick it up then." He slipped out as quickly as he'd entered.

Stifling another yawn, she took a longer drink from her mug. Then she shuffled things around on her desk so she had a bit of space to lay out the printed pages of her draft article. Huff had already been through it, writing his questions and comments in the margins. On the first page was his main comment, one that annoyed her to no end.

Your story is good, but not compelling. Something is missing, something to hook the reader.

As far as she was concerned, the story had a built-in hook: the exorbitant amount of money the city had paid Ken to take on the Grand Pearl project. After all, that was what had gotten the executives excited about the story and why they'd requested the feature in the first place. Huff had obviously bought into that, because he'd mentioned it when he'd first assigned her the article.

No, something else was at play here. She and Huff had worked together for nine and a half years, and he'd edited everything she'd written for the paper. She suspected that Huff had read the draft and immediately known that she had more information than she was including in the story. While that was true, she'd made a promise to Ken. The details of his family's past were simply out of the question. If she betrayed him now, he'd never trust her again.

Taking a deep breath to steel herself for the work ahead, she grabbed her favorite editing pen and began poring over her pages once again. She read through every page for what felt like the fiftieth time, making her notes around Huff's. The bright green ink of her pen stood out in contrast to the red notations Huff had made earlier and made her pages look like a Christmas display in a store window.

When she'd done a complete run-through of the pages, she opened her laptop and pulled up the old document. Incorporating her notes along with those of her editor, she banged out a second draft. It took a while before she deemed it ready to be reviewed. But by the time she finally sent the article to her wireless printer, she felt pretty confident that she'd turned out a much better version of her original story. She retrieved the freshly printed pages, clipping them together the way Huff preferred. Setting them on the corner of her desk, she swiped the screen of her phone to see if she'd missed any texts.

Damn. Four thirty already? She'd been working so hard on the article that she hadn't realized how much time had passed. She blew out a breath. At least that meant the end of the workday was finally in sight.

She grabbed a granola bar from her desk drawer. While she munched, she looked forward to the end of the day. She'd worked incredibly hard today and was on the verge of total mental exhaustion. Days like this drained her and fueled the feelings of burnout she felt brewing inside. She had no idea how many more years of this she would be able to take. The deadlines, the responsibility for other staffers and the near-constant threat of being laid off were weighing heavily on her shoulders.

She thought of Ken and the way he shrugged most things off. He was cool, collected and aloof. At first she'd found those qualities annoying, but now she was willing to admit that she could use a bit more calm in her life.

A wicked smile tilted the corners of her mouth as she thought of a way to calm her nerves and add a little spice to this otherwise crazy day. Opening a text message to Ken, she started typing.

I'm super stressed. Could really use a massage.

She hit Send. Determined not to wait for his reply like an overeager teenager, she set the phone down on the corner of her desk and started straightening up in preparation for going home.

The phone buzzed a few seconds later.

She picked it up, checked Ken's reply.

Should I use my hands? Or something else?

Her body temperature rose fifteen degrees the moment she read his message. It amazed her how he could be so laid-back and yet so incredibly sexy. Her mind traveled back to that night in his garden when his touch had awakened every nerve ending in her body. Her tongue darted out to swipe over her lower lip as she typed a response.

Use everything at your disposal.

She didn't even have time to put the phone down before his response came.

Come to my office and I will.

The hairs on the back of her neck stood on end, and her nipples tightened beneath the fabric of the simple A-line dress she'd worn to work. Slipping the phone into her purse, she hurried to gather her things. It was a quarter till five, but she didn't plan on hanging around any longer than she had to.

She was on her way out the door when she saw Porter headed toward her.

"Oh, Ms. Gregory. I was just on my way to pick up your revision…"

"It's on my desk," she called as she blew past him. "Lock the door behind you."

"Will do." Porter moved on.

As she turned the corner, she saw Porter coming out of her office with her article pages.

"Hey, Ken. I'm leaving."

Ken looked up from his computer to see Lynn standing in his office door. It was a little after five, and he was still busy rendering a sketch into a blueprint with the software program.

"Okay. Are the interns already gone?"

She nodded. "Left about an hour ago. When are you leaving?"

He shrugged. "I've hit a snag with this sketch. For some reason the software isn't creating the blueprint correctly. I'm going to hang around for a bit, see if I can figure it out."

"Isn't the band playing tonight?"

"Yeah. So if I don't get it right in the next half hour, it will have to wait until tomorrow."

"Well, don't work too hard. See you in the morning." She then slipped out.

The office suite was so quiet, he could hear Lynn's retreating footsteps as well as the sound of the main entrance door opening and shutting as she left. Once he was alone, he ran a hand over his tired eyes. Grabbing a bottle of water from the small cooler by his desk, he turned his attention back to his computer.

He was so engrossed in trying to figure out the glitch he didn't hear the door open a few minutes later. But he did hear footsteps in the hallway. When his ears picked up the distinctive *click-click* of a woman's high-heeled shoes on the tile floor, he looked up, watching the door expectantly. *Maybe Lynn forgot something.*

Nona appeared at the door instead. She wore her hair down around her shoulders, and her body was draped in a muted red dress. The short sleeves and knee-length design of the garment meant that a good deal of her bronze skin was visible to his appreciative eyes. Gold studs sparkled in her ears, mirroring the desire dancing in her brown eyes.

He smiled, closing the software program. Whatever was wrong with it could wait. "It's good to see you."

"It's even better to see you." She slowly moved toward his desk. "I'm sorry we haven't been able to get together this past week. I've missed you."

"I've missed you, too." He couldn't take his eyes off the tempting sway of her hips and the long, dark legs moving in his direction. He started to rise from his seat.

She reached him before he could get up and stopped him with an open palm on his chest. "Don't get up on my account, baby."

He flopped back down in the chair, mesmerized. "Whatever you say." He watched her, realizing for the first time that she was holding something inside a clenched fist. Before he could ask her what it was, she opened her hand and unfurled it.

He groaned when he saw what it was.

Holding up the tiny pair of thong underwear so he could see it, she then folded them neatly. "I think these belong to you." She tucked the tiny triangle of red fabric into the front pocket of his button-down shirt.

"Nona." All he could do was say her name as she raised the hem of her dress and straddled his lap. Arousal roared through him, his manhood stretching and straining against the zipper of his trousers.

She settled in, purring. "Ooh. You're so ready for me." She leaned forward, draping her arms around his neck.

He was utterly outdone and way past turned on. Having Nona on his lap, naked from the waist down, was slowly pushing him toward the absolute limit of his self-control. His hands found their way to her naked flesh, and he filled his palms with the round softness of her bottom. Leaning into her, he inhaled the sweet fragrance clinging to her skin and hair. "God, you're wicked."

"Only for you, boo. I've never done anything like this before." Her fingertips stroked over his jaw.

"I have a show tonight," he managed while staring down the front of her dress into her cleavage. Desire raged through him like a five-alarm forest fire, and he was so hard he doubted he'd be able to stand, let alone walk. For the first time ever, he gave serious consideration to ditching the show.

She twisted her face into a mock pout. "You still have a little time, don't you?"

"Not enough for what I want to do to you." He kissed

her, pressing his lips against hers while he moved one of his hands through her hair. As their tongues mated and danced, all he could think about was turning her around, bending her over his desk and taking her until she screamed.

They spent a few moments wrapped up in the potency of the kiss, their hands roving each other's bodies. When she finally drew away, her breath came in short little gasps.

"I need a little something, baby. It was rough day." She fixed him with a sexy stare.

He had way more than a little something for her. But he knew turning her hips up over his desk would be asking for trouble. His desk was covered with things tied to the Grand Pearl project. There was no time to properly put away his sketches and renderings, and as much as he wanted her, he didn't want to ruin several days' work. "Then we need to get out of here, quick."

"Your shows are still at the Blue Lounge?"

He nodded while tracing the outline of her nipple through the fabric of her dress.

She released a low moan as she rose from his lap. Standing, she tugged the dress back down over her hips. "Let's go to my place. I only live about twenty minutes from there."

She'd just provided a much better solution than going all the way out to his house, which was far outside the city limits. Catching hold of her hand, he lifted himself from the chair. Walking in his current state of desire was uncomfortable at best, but somehow, he managed. Once he'd gathered his things, shut off the lights and locked up, he followed her out of the office suite.

Chapter 15

As Nona unlocked the front door of her cottage in the Elizabeth section of the city, she was very aware of Ken's presence. His warm breath was on her neck, and his arms were draped around her waist possessively. When she entered the house, he followed her step for step, still holding her.

Sheba, having heard the door open, ran up the moment Nona dropped her keys in the ceramic bowl by the door. Nona squirmed out of Ken's embrace long enough to stoop and give the dog's head a rub. "Hey, girl." She looked up at Ken. "Go on into my room and get comfortable while I take care of her. It's the second door on the right." She pointed.

"Don't be too long." He leaned down to kiss her forehead before slipping past her.

"Oh, I won't." She appreciated her vantage point, eye level with his ass in dark denim jeans, as he walked away.

She got Sheba outside, back in and fed in record time, then closed her companion up in the spare bedroom for the evening. She didn't want an audience for what she and Ken were about to do.

When she entered her bedroom, she found him sitting on the edge of her bed. Glad she'd made it up this morning, she walked over to him. Her steps were slow and purposefully seductive.

When she was close enough for him to reach her, he pulled her into his arms and placed his lips against her. She wrapped her arms around his neck, letting the kiss deepen. His tongue stroked the inner corners of her mouth, and her blood heated as the desire she'd felt in his office rose anew, hotter and stronger than before. She was about to climb into his lap when he pulled back.

"What is it?" She hoped he hadn't changed his mind and decided he didn't have time before the show after all. After the day she'd had, she needed him to make it all better.

"I had something else in mind." He pointed behind her.

It took a moment for her to figure out what he meant. But when her eyes landed on the armchair and ottoman in the corner of her room, she smiled. Turning back toward him, she pursed her lips. "Ken, you naughty boy."

"I'm not sorry. You're the one who came to my office and tucked a thong into my pocket." He pointed to the chair.

She strolled over to it, awaiting his next instructions.

"Go stand behind it."

She did as instructed, and while she sensed what he'd ask her to do next, she waited. She wanted to hear him say it.

He was on his feet now, unfastening his pants as he moved toward her. "Bend over it, honey."

With a smile, she did as he asked. Since she wasn't wearing any panties, she could feel the breeze that caressed her intimately as she turned her hips up over the back of the chair. Her dress slid up a couple of inches due to her positioning.

A few seconds later, he wedged himself into the space between the wall and her upturned ass. He drew in a breath through clenched teeth, and she smiled, knowing he liked what he saw.

"Mmm. Nona." He pushed her dress all the way up until it bunched around her stomach, then palmed her backside with a slow, gentle caress. "When we were in my office, all I could think about was bending you over my desk."

She sighed in response to his touch and his words. She could not remember ever wanting someone this much, but that seemed to be the effect he had on her. He drove her absolutely mad with desire.

The next sound she heard was rustling around as he got a condom from his pocket. Seconds later, she felt his sheathed manhood probing her.

"Yes, baby." She settled into her position, bracing for what was to come.

With a growl, he slid inside her. His hands came

around to cup her breasts, and she arched her back. The pleasure made her coo and sigh, and soon she was moving her hips in time with his thrusts, meeting him stroke for stroke.

It wasn't long before their mingled shouts and moans filled the room. She screamed his name as orgasm flashed through her body like lightning, and his completion followed close behind.

For a few moments, they both lay slumped over the back of her wing chair. In the silence, Nona realized that Ken had claimed her heart, and there was no way of getting it back.

She loved him, and she probably had since the night they'd first made love. But now she had to figure out the right time and the right way to tell him.

Later, as Ken lay next to Nona in her bed, he looked at the glowing red numbers of the digital clock on her nightstand. He had forty-five minutes to be dressed and onstage at the Blue Lounge. Thankfully, he'd brought his stage clothes with him to work that day, having anticipated working late and going straight to the club from his office.

He shifted in bed, waking Nona. What was supposed to be a quickie had turned into two consecutive hot and heavy lovemaking sessions. After he'd taken her from behind, she'd brought him back to the bed and climbed on top of him. Because he couldn't deny her, he'd let her continue until they were both climaxing again.

If he had a choice, he would remain in bed with her all night, showing her all the many ways he could keep her entertained. But his commitment to the band wouldn't allow it. "Honey, we have to get up. I have to be at the lounge soon."

She stuck out her bottom lip in a mock pout.

"I know. But I have to get going." He gave her bottom a possessive squeeze, then rose from the bed.

"I guess I'd better get up, too, if I'm going to the show." She rolled out of bed and padded naked to her closet.

He threw on his slacks, not bothering with any other article of his strewn clothing, and jogged outside. He retrieved the bag holding his stage clothes and brought it inside.

Back in Nona's bedroom, he stuck his head into the closet. "Mind if I take a shower?"

She shook her head. "No. Go ahead."

What followed was the quickest shower of his life, and she entered the bathroom as he stepped out. She took her shower while he threw on his underwear, slacks and shirt. Checking the time, he saw that he'd have to put the rest of it on at the club.

Soon, they were both in Nona's driveway, getting into their respective vehicles.

"Ken?" She was standing in the space between her open car door and the cabin of her sedan.

Seated in the driver seat of his car, he looked toward her. "What is it?"

"What's happening between us? What are we doing?"

He shrugged, not knowing if she was ready to hear

that he loved her. "Seeing each other, enjoying each other's company. I don't really care what we call it."

She nodded, but she didn't look terribly reassured.

He started his engine, because if he didn't leave in the next five minutes, he'd be late for sound check. "My father once told me that a man can never be sure he loves a woman until she hurts him."

A crooked smile crossed her face. "But I would never hurt you, Ken."

He winked at her. "I know. I'll see you at the club."

Putting the car in Reverse, he backed out of the driveway.

Chapter 16

Jogging to her seat at a table near the stage, Nona slid into it. Three other women were already seated there, and she remembered Ken telling her she'd be sitting with the wives of his bandmates. Feeling somewhat giddy to get a seat at the table of honor, she smiled at her tablemates. "Hi, ladies. I'm Nona."

The woman closest to her, brown skinned with a sleek bob, extended her hand. "Hello, there. I'm Eve, Darius's wife." She gestured to the slightly darker-skinned woman with the cute short do sitting to her right. "This is Rashad's wife, Lina, and next to her is Joi, Marco's wife."

Lina smiled. "Hey, girl."

Joi raised her hand, wiggling French-manicured fingertips in her direction. "Welcome to our little crew."

"It's nice to meet all of you." Nona settled into the leather cushion of the chair, hanging the strap of her small handbag on the backrest. Now that she was finally seated after the mad dash to make it there on time, she took deep breaths and tried to slow her racing heartbeat.

A giggle sounded next to her, and she looked over at Eve.

"I'm not trying to get in your business, but are you okay? You seem a little…out of breath." Eve's eyes held a mixture of concern and curiosity.

Sucking in her bottom lip, Nona blinked a few times. *Am I that obvious?* "Don't mind me. I'll be fine. Really."

Lina, taking a sip from the bright red mixed drink in front of her, said sagely, "Oh, honey, trust me. We get it. No judgment from us."

Joi added, "You know what they say about birds of a feather. All of our husbands are a lot to handle, so we can only assume the same is true of Ken."

An outdone Nona could only smile. Even though she'd just met the ladies, she could tell they would get along fine. "I appreciate that. Now, who do I talk to about getting one of those fruity drinks?"

"I got you, girl." Lina raised her hand into the air. "Pierre, can you come here for a minute, boo?"

Shortly a fair-skinned man of average height, wearing black slacks, a white shirt and a blue vest, appeared next to their table. "What can I get you?"

Lina gestured toward Nona. "Can you hook our sista up with something sweet?"

Nona looked toward the waiter. "I'd love a Harvey Wallbanger, light on the liquor."

"You got it." The smiling Pierre disappeared through the maze of crowded tables.

"They should be raising the curtain any minute." Joi ran a hand through the dark waves of her hair. "Does anybody know what they're playing tonight?"

Eve shrugged. "Darius didn't say anything to me about it."

Stirring her drink, Lina crinkled her brow. "I think Rashad said something about them playing a tribute to Lena Horne. It's her birthday."

Nona turned toward the stage, eager to hear the set. Not only did she love Lena Horne, but she loved the idea that the Gents, as an all-male jazz quartet, would decide to pay tribute to her.

Eve raised her glass. Turning Lina's way, she quipped, "Here's hoping your husband can hit the notes, girl."

Lina answered with a playful punch to Eve's upper arm, but everyone at the table giggled.

Pierre placed Nona's drink on the table and slipped away quickly.

The house lights were lowered then, and a hush fell over the room as the emcee came out to announce the band. Once he'd made his introduction, the blue velvet curtain was raised. Nona took in the sight of the band and was immediately impressed. Their stage costumes for the night consisted of navy blue suits tailored to fit each man's body. Beneath the suits, each man wore a coal-black shirt and a metallic silver tie. Black dress shoes and black fedoras with silver bands completed their look.

Naturally, Nona's eyes went right to Ken, who was seated near the rear of the stage behind his drum set. She licked her lips as her eyes feasted on her tasty morsel of a man. He looked so fine, it was all she could do to remain in her seat. She wanted to climb up on the lip of the stage, stroll over to that stool he was sitting on and peel that sexy suit off him one article at a time.

In the darkness, she heard Eve say, "Yes, Lord. I love it when they clean up for a show."

Every woman at the table made a sound of agreement in response. If there were four better-looking men on Earth, Nona would be surprised.

Ken raised his sticks into the air, tapping them together. "One and a two and a…"

On cue, the men began playing their instruments. A few notes later, Nona recognized the tune.

Rashad, his hands on the keys, leaned forward to sing into the microphone set up next to the piano.

For the next several minutes, Nona and everyone else in the lounge were graced with Rashad's rendition of "Stormy Weather." While he modified the vocals and lyrics slightly to fit the pitch and timbre of his voice, he remained true to the mood of the tune. Tapping her toe beneath the table, Nona could tell that Rashad was a fantastic vocalist. Despite Eve's cheeky comment, Rashad wasn't having any trouble hitting the notes.

After they finished the song and waited for the thunderous applause to go down, the band segued into "Wives and Lovers," another song Ms. Horne had recorded. Next came "Singing in the Rain," and by the time the Gents started "Moon River," they'd won Nona over as a new fan.

She was so busy enjoying the music that she barely noticed her phone buzzing. Taking it from her handbag, she unlocked it and checked the screen. An email awaited her from Huff, and while she generally wouldn't check work email at a moment like this, something told her it was important.

She opened the email, while still bopping her head. Her eyes scanned the message from her boss.

Nona, thanks for revising the article, and for adding in the missing piece! The drama with Ken's family makes for a very compelling read and I'm sure...

Nona's eyes grew large. *What the hell is he talking about?* She read on, hoping to find the answer to that question.

When Porter brought me your notebook with the revised pages, I didn't understand at first. But since you provided the information, I took the liberty of adding it to your article...

Holy. Shit. The notebook in question had to be her journal. She hadn't seen it in a few days, and now she surmised that she must have brought it to work by mistake. Porter probably hadn't realized he'd picked it up with her article and delivered it to her boss. And knowing Huff, he probably felt very proud of himself right now. After all, he'd gotten the scoop, and that was his top priority.

She panicked. Looking toward Ken, who was still onstage behind the drum set, she knew she needed to warn him. Feature articles normally appeared on the newspaper's website at one minute past midnight on the day of publication. It was now twenty minutes after eleven. Based on the way the boys were jamming, she didn't think the show would end any time soon.

She tapped Eve's shoulder, and asked, "How long do the shows usually last?"

"Oh, they go on until midnight, twelve thirty most of the time." Eve shimmied in her seat, obviously enjoying the music.

Closing her eyes, Nona cursed under her breath.

Leaving her untouched drink and her purse, she got up from the table and dashed toward the backstage corridor.

Ken lifted his sticks above his head, twirling them like two miniature batons before returning to the ride cymbal and the snare. Throwing a little flair into his performances kept him from getting bored and kept the audience engaged during transitions.

Rashad said into the microphone, "Y'all give it up for Ken Yamada, the drum man with the plan!"

The crowd ate it up, giving a rousing cheer. Ken smiled as he kept playing, enjoying his moment in the spotlight. Not only was Rashad the vocalist and the pianist, he also served as the band's hype man. His personality lent itself to the job, and Ken couldn't imagine anyone else doing it.

He could feel the perspiration gathering beneath the band of his fedora. Being under the stage lights usually led to him overheating about halfway through a set. With a quick motion of his right hand, he used the tip of one of his sticks to knock the hat off. It landed on the floor to the right of his stool and he kept playing without missing a beat.

A rustle of movement in the wings caught his attention. Keeping his focus on the drums, he gave a sidelong glance to his far right. He thought he saw Nona there, waving and gesturing wildly. Unable to stop at this point in the song, he turned his attention back to his fast-flying sticks.

During the applause break when the song ended, he turned his head. Confusion knit his brow as he caught sight of Nona, waving her arms like an air traffic controller on the flight line. *What is she doing?*

Her eyes were large, and she was mouthing something, but he couldn't hear her over the applause or make out what she was trying to say. Gesturing to let her know he couldn't hear her, he positioned his sticks for the start of the next song.

A security guard appeared behind Nona, and she quit flailing. As the guard led her away, Ken scratched his head. *What was that all about?* He could tell she wanted something, and he hated to put her off. But whatever it was, it would have to wait until the show ended. As he often reminded his bandmates, his drumming provided the foundation for everything they played. Without him, they'd be completely lost.

He got his head back in the game, concentrating fully on the music. He got into a groove, and as the last song of the night's set ended, he leaned into his drum set and kept playing. As Rashad, Darius and Marco set their instruments aside, Ken played an epic drum solo that went on a good three or four minutes. For that brief period, he felt weightless, blissful, as if the drum gods were smiling on him and lending him their collective powers. When he threw his sticks to the stage floor, the entire room full of people jumped to their feet for a thunderous ovation. When Ken looked around, even his bandmates were applauding.

As the excitement died down, Ken got up from his stool and retrieved the hat he'd tossed earlier. When he stood up with the hat in his hand, Nona was there again, standing in the wings at stage right.

This time, as he got a good look at her, he could see the fat puddles of water standing in her eyes. Her face was wet, streaked with tears she'd already shed, and her eyes held profound sadness.

Concern gripped him, and he grabbed his sticks and rushed to her side. "Nona. Baby, you've been crying. What's wrong?"

Her answering sob tugged at his heart.

He gathered her in his arms. "Come on. Let's go backstage where we can talk." With his arm draped around her trembling shoulders, he led her through the performers' area of the lounge to one of the empty dressing rooms. He closed the door behind them as they entered.

The room was sparsely furnished. A lighted vanity and matching bench occupied one wall, while a tan leather love seat occupied the opposite wall. A short-legged wooden coffee table centered the space.

She flopped down on the love seat, and he sat next to her.

Looking into her watery eyes, he gave her hand a squeeze. "Now, tell me what's wrong."

She shifted her gaze away from him, as if unable to meet his eyes.

He persisted. "I'm not going anywhere until you tell me what the problem is."

"It's too late. It's just too late." She shook her head back and forth as she whispered the words.

"Too late? What are you talking about?"

A deep sigh.

"Nona."

"I don't know how to tell you this, but…" Her hands were in her lap, and she wrung them.

He'd never seen her act this way, and it dawned on him that whatever she was about to say must be pretty bad. Rather than press her any further, he waited.

A few long, silent minutes ticked by before she spoke. "What you told me about your family. Your mother's affair. Your sister. Your father's efforts to hide it all. I made a mistake and now it's in my feature article."

His heart stopped. He blinked a few times. "You're not serious."

"I wish it weren't true, but it is." She was staring at her hands now where they rested in her lap.

He moved away from her, as far as he could until he bumped into the arm of the love seat. "But the newspaper isn't out yet. You can stop…"

She shook her head. "The online version goes live at midnight."

He didn't need to check the time to know that midnight had come and gone. He guessed it was around one o'clock in the morning by now.

"Listen, I write in a personal journal. Sort of like a diary. I think it must have gotten mixed up with my work papers and…"

He wasn't interested in her meandering explanation. "Stop." A wave of emotion came over him, strong and all consuming. It was probably the worst feeling he'd ever experienced. "So this is how it feels."

"What?" She appeared confused.

"This is how it feels to be betrayed by the woman you love. I would say it's like a knife in my heart, but it's worse than that. Much worse." His words were honest and edged with the bitterness he felt. He would much rather have been slapped across the face than to be standing here with her now, knowing she'd sold him out this way.

Her eyes grew wide, filling again with tears. "Did you just say you love me?"

He stood, his hands curled tightly at his sides. "I did. But that was when I thought I could trust you." Turning, he started to walk away. He needed to get out of this tiny room and away from this woman who'd stolen his heart, learned his secrets and then used them against him.

"Ken, wait. This was all a mistake."

He didn't stop, didn't respond. Grabbing the door-knob, he yanked the door open.

"Please, Ken! Please. I love you, too." Her voice was thick with tears.

He heard her words coming from behind him, heard the emotion. Without turning around, he spoke. "If we don't have trust, we don't have anything."

And with that, he walked out, not bothering to look back.

Chapter 17

Nona strode into the newspaper building Thursday morning, bypassing her office and heading straight for Wendell's. Instead of taking the time and care she usually did before coming into work, she'd rolled out of bed, thrown on a white tee and a pair of cutoff shorts, and made her way to work.

The door to her boss's office was already open, and he looked up the minute she stepped inside. His brow furrowed with confusion and concern when he saw her. "Nona? I'd say good morning, but you look like hell. What's wrong?"

Walking over to his desk, she rested her palms on the edge. "Huff, why did you publish the things in my journal as part of my feature?"

"What?"

She frowned, waited.

He leaned back in his chair, his expression changing. "Porter turned in a stack of papers that was supposed to be your article. The notebook was in between the pages, so…" He shrugged.

"So you used information from my private journal, without my permission."

"Obviously it's not all that private, because you brought it to work." He gestured to the corner of his desk. "It's over there if you want it."

She snatched the notebook and tucked it into her purse. "I can't believe you, Huff. Reading my journal is pretty low, but including that information in the story, with my name on it? Outrageous."

He tented his fingers. "It's like I told you, the story wasn't compelling. I knew you were holding back when I read your first draft. You should thank me, really. I made your first front-page feature unforgettable. Do you realize what an amazing scoop this was?"

She could feel the excitement rolling off him, and in another time and place, she might have felt that way, too. He was right: the article was unforgettable. But if she couldn't convince Ken that she'd made a mistake, that she hadn't set out to purposefully betray him, it would be unforgettable for all the wrong reasons. "You know, I've waited a long time for a front-page feature. But now that I have it, it doesn't even matter. The cost was too high."

His face changed, and for the first time since she'd entered, she saw a modicum of sympathy. "I'm assuming this had put you on bad terms with Mr. Yamada."

You don't know the half of it. "'Bad terms' is a gross understatement of what happened between us. Although I'm sure you don't care."

"Come on, Nona. I do care, because I genuinely like you and respect you as a colleague."

She stood, folded her arms over her chest. "Good. Then you'll respect me when I say I won't be staying today, and that I'll be taking some of my vacation days."

He frowned. "How long are you going to be gone?"

"I have about three weeks of vacation days banked, so I don't know. But I can tell you that you won't see me before Monday." And when she did come back, she knew it might just be so she could clean out her office. But she didn't tell him that then—she had some serious thinking to do.

He nodded, though he didn't seem overly pleased. "I can understand that. Go ahead and take some time, but try to get back as soon as you can. The executive board is very pleased with the story, and they'll want to speak to you about more features."

She sighed, knowing that just a week ago, she would have considered that great news. "'Bye, Huff."

If he had anything else to say, she didn't want to hear it, so she didn't wait around. Within fifteen minutes, she was in her car, on the highway heading east. Like any other time she had a problem or needed to get away, she was headed to Sapphire Shores to hide out.

Two and a half hours later, she used her spare key to let herself in to Hadley's cottage. She'd texted Hadley to let her know she was coming so she wouldn't come home from work to a surprise houseguest. Hadley had a key to Nona's house as well, although she had yet to use it. Both women agreed that Hadley possessed the more desirable home, at least as far as location was concerned.

After tossing her bags into the guest bedroom, Nona went into the kitchen. Despite the hot, humid day outside, the interior of Hadley's spacious cottage felt cool and comfortable. The air-conditioning unit got an assist from the many rattan ceiling fans hanging in the rafters. The main area of the house alone had four fans, and they were all turning at the moment.

Nona fixed herself a cup of hot green tea, adding a touch of sugar and lemon. Then she retreated to the front of Hadley's living room, where two wide wicker armchairs faced the front window. Dropping onto the floral cushion of one of the chairs, she curled up with her tea.

The house was situated on a wide strip of grass that soon gave way to sand and the churning waters of the Atlantic. There were at most three hundred yards between Nona's spot in the window and the edge of the water. She sipped from the mug, feeling a degree of calm wash over her.

She didn't realize she'd fallen asleep until Hadley's gentle shake woke her. "I can't believe you screwed things up with Ken that fast. This has to be a record." She plopped down in the matching chair and fixed Nona with a probing stare.

Blinking a few times, Nona stretched and repositioned herself in the chair. "Neither can I. I can't believe I made the mistake of taking my journal to work.

But if I hadn't, I guess I never would have known what kind of person Huff really is."

Shaking her head, Hadley spoke. "This isn't about Huff or any of those other fools at the paper. This is about you and, to a lesser degree, Ken. When are you going to give up that job, girl? We both know you should be teaching dance full-time."

"You know my mom wouldn't have that."

"Girl, you just turned thirty-four. I know you love your mama and everything but jeez. You're a grown woman. Live your life!"

In her mind's eye, Nona could see the smiling faces of her students. She loved dancing, and she loved knowing that her instruction not only passed on an art form she loved to a younger generation but had a positive impact on their lives. "You're right. I'm tired of dealing with the politics at the paper. Teaching dance brings me joy."

"Of course I'm right. And make sure you tell my brothers that before you go back to Charlotte. They don't think I know much about anything." She pursed her lips, the same way she always did when speaking of them.

"That's only half my problem, though. What about Ken? How can I get him back when he doesn't trust me anymore?" She sighed. He'd only been in her life for three short weeks, but it had still hurt like hell to lose him.

Hadley shrugged. "Hell if I know. But I do know he's made you the happiest I've ever seen you. So you better figure something out. Just think about it. You know how you lost his trust. What can you do to get it back?"

"I don't know." She directed her gaze back toward the water. "I just don't know."

"Well, the good news is, you can stay here and stare at the water until you figure it out." Hadley climbed to her feet. "I'm going to take a shower. I'll be back in a few."

"Okay."

As Hadley walked away, leaving Nona alone with her thoughts, she inhaled deeply.

Whatever it took, she would convince Ken that she could be trusted and that what they shared was too precious to throw away.

Friday night, Ken found himself back at Miyu's apartment. When he'd been with his sister last, they'd been joking and teasing each other. As he sat on the white sofa in her living room now, absently staring in the direction of the television, the mood was much more subdued, even solemn.

After he'd left the Blue Lounge in the wee hours of the previous morning, he'd called to inform his father of the article's publication. Hiro being awake at that hour wasn't a surprise, since the old man often stayed up past two and slept in until noon. When Ken had asked his father why he was up at such odd hours, his reply had been simple.

"Old age."

Hiro had been grim but resigned when he heard the news, as if he'd fully expected his secrets to get out one day. Ken, on the other hand, still struggled to process what had happened. He just couldn't figure out how Nona could have done such a thing. He hadn't read more than the first paragraph of the article, because he couldn't bring himself go any further. The headline alone had been enough to do him in: Local Artist Overcomes Family Scandal to Achieve Coveted Restoration Project.

When he'd seen the headline in print, he could only shake his head. Nona had approached him to write a story about his process, and somehow the finished article had ended up putting the spotlight on one of the most difficult episodes in his past. Pushing aside thoughts of Nona and the sensationalized crap she called an article, he put his focus on his baby sister.

Miyu sat on the opposite end of the sofa from him, with her short legs tucked beneath her bottom. She wore a red-and-white NC State T-shirt with a pair of red track pants bearing a white stripe. Her hair was tucked up into another messy ponytail, and her eyes were fixed on the television screen. She'd been watching some inane reality show since he'd arrived, and from what Ken could tell, the show had her full interest and attention.

But after several minutes of silence, she turned his way. "Ken, what's up with you? You look like someone died." She paused, cocked her head to the side. "Is something wrong with Hiro?"

"Not in the physical sense." He scratched his chin as he wondered how to broach the subject of the article with her. "He's upset, but I think he'll eventually calm down."

"Is this about the article in the paper, where they talk about Mom and me?"

Ken's gaze shifted to meet his sister's eyes. "Yes. You speak very casually about all of this."

She shrugged. "I see no reason to get upset."

He tried to think of a way to say it that would make sense to her. "My father is very concerned with image, with saving face. Having the world know about you, and how you got here, makes him very uncomfortable."

"I get that, and he's entitled to his feelings. But I'm also entitled to not let it bother me."

He stared at her. "Miyu, why isn't this upsetting you? Not that I want you to be upset, because you know I'd do anything to protect you. I just don't understand your reasoning here."

She scooted a bit closer to him. "Ken, I always knew Hiro wasn't my father. From the time I could speak, he asked me to call him by his first name, even though you called him Dad. He never connected with me, never made any effort to bond, or to get to know me even. You and Frances did everything for me."

He said nothing, content to listen to what she had to say.

"Plus, there's the obvious difference in my appearance. My skin is darker than yours and Hiro's, and my hair has a different texture. The signs were everywhere, telling me that I didn't fit in with you and Hiro. Did you really think that if you never said it out loud, I'd never notice?"

"I guess I was so busy protecting you that I never

stopped to think about your perception of the situation. You've always been smart, Miyu."

"It isn't an ideal situation, but is what it is. I wish I had gotten a chance to know Mom, and it's unfortunate that my being around made things difficult for Hiro. Regardless of any of that, I'm here. God saw fit to give me life, so I'm just going to make the best of it and try to help someone else along the way."

In that moment, he realized he hadn't been giving his sister nearly enough credit. She was smart, insightful and intuitive. His heart swelled with pride, because she possessed a wisdom well beyond her twenty-one years. "I'm sorry, Miyu. I know it isn't my place to apologize for the way my father treated you. But I can say I'm sorry for the way I've been acting."

A soft smile crossed her face. "You don't have anything to be sorry about, Kenny. I know you're overprotective because you love me so much. And I love you right back." She moved over until she was next to him, placed her arms around his shoulders and hugged him. "Thank you for everything you've done for me."

He returned the hug. "Before Mom got pregnant, I'd been asking for a baby sister. I never would have guessed I'd get one under those circumstances. I'm just happy my wish came true." He held her for a few seconds before releasing her.

"Are you sure Hiro's going to be okay?" She had genuine concern in her eyes.

Ken admired the way she always asked about Hiro, showing much more care for him than he ever had for her. He rumpled her hair. "I think so. It might help if you came to the house with me, though. I think the three of us should sit down and talk about this thing."

"I agree. That's a conversation that's long overdue." She settled back into her favorite position and returned to watching television.

Watching her, Ken smiled. Considering the environment she'd come from, Miyu was remarkably well adjusted. If his father could release his bitterness, he would probably be similarly impressed with the child his late wife had left behind.

An image of Nona popped into his mind. He cringed, not wanting to think about her. Thinking about her meant exploring the pain she'd made him feel. She'd demonstrated precisely why he'd never allowed himself to get seriously involved with a woman. He'd always suspected that sharing his heart and his life with someone would leave him open, vulnerable to whatever harm she might do to him. With Nona, things had turned out just as he feared.

Determined to get his mind off Nona and whatever feelings he'd thought he harbored for her, he shifted in his seat. Draping his arm over the back of the sofa, Ken settled in and tried to take an interest in the show his sister watched.

Without looking away from the TV, she asked, "Kenny, did you read the article?"

He shook his head. "No, and I don't plan to."

"You should read it. I know you're mad with the writer. But if you read it, you'd learn something."

"And what's that?"

Miyu met his eyes. "She loves you, Kenny. Only

someone who loves you would write about you like that."

He wasn't sure he believed her.

"Just read it." And she lapsed back into silence.

Ken groaned, knowing that he would probably read it now that his sister had pressed him.

And he wasn't sure he was ready for what he might find.

Chapter 18

When Nona let herself in to her parents' house Monday evening, she found them both sitting in the living room. Her mother was engrossed in a magazine while her father watched cable news on the television. Steeling herself for a confrontation, she entered the house fully and closed the door behind her. "Hey, Mommy, hey, Daddy."

Gordon looked up first. "Hey, Nonie. What a nice surprise."

"What are you doing here, baby? I can't remember the last time you came over on a Monday." Aretha folded the page of her magazine to mark her place then closed it and set it aside.

"I just wanted to talk to you both, and it's important.

I thought it would be better to come over than to call." She sat down on the sofa next to her mother.

"Before you do, I just want to say how proud I am of you." A bright smile lit her mother's face. "Seeing your byline on the front page last week was really something. And I read the article, too. It was fantastic, though it really is sad what happened with Ken's mother."

Nona sighed.

Her face crinkled in confusion, Aretha asked, "Is there something wrong? That's not the reaction I usually get when I compliment your writing."

"Thanks for the compliment, Mommy. I'm glad it made you happy, even though I can't say I'm proud of the article."

Now Aretha looked even more confused. "Nona, you're going to have to tell me what's going on."

She blew out a breath. Not seeing any reason to prolong what was sure to be an awkward conversation, she spit it out. "I resigned my position at the paper today, Mommy. I gave my two weeks' notice, and I'm going to use my vacation time so I don't have to go back."

"What? Why would you do that, just when you're so close to getting that promotion?" Aretha fixed her daughter with a disappointed expression.

"I'm sorry, Mommy. I know you're surprised and disappointed, but this has been coming for a long time. I just don't feel the same way about journalism as I used to. It doesn't excite me anymore."

"But Nona, you were doing so well at the paper. You were going to be editor in chief one day." Aretha's tone and expression revealed that she still clung to those long-held dreams for her daughter's future.

Nona had wanted that once, too. Over the past few days, though, she'd achieved a new degree of clarity. Now she knew that the editor-in-chief position had never been her dream as much as remnants of her mother's own past ambitions. "I don't want that anymore, Mommy. In terms of job stress, the cost is simply too high. And while this feature article impressed some folks, it has blown up in my face, big-time."

Gordon broke his silence. "Let me guess. Mr. Yamada asked you not to write about his family drama, didn't he?"

"Yes. And if I hadn't made the mistake of taking my journal to work, those things would have never made it into the finished article. I had every intention of doing as he asked. I don't even know when my journal got mixed up with my stuff, and now I'm royally screwed because of it."

"Because you care about him." Her father made a statement instead of asking a question.

She nodded. "I do. But now I think I've lost him."

"Wait a minute. Are you saying you quit your job because of the architect you were writing about?" Aretha was obviously still unclear on her daughter's motivations.

"Ken does play a role in this, because of the article. Mommy, at the heart of this, it isn't about Ken or anybody else. It's about me." She grabbed her mother's hand. "I'm not happy working at the newspaper anymore."

Her frown deepened. "And I suppose you're going to tell me you're happy teaching dance."

"And what's wrong with that, Rethie?" Gordon chimed in, addressing his wife. "She's a grown woman. She's got enough sense to know what she wants."

"But Gordon, she should—"

"She should do whatever she wants." Gordon eased forward in his seat. "It's high time you stop pressuring her to follow *your* dream."

Aretha drew back, lowered her gaze.

Gordon's voice softened as he spoke again. "Rethie, you know I love you. And I love our daughter. You two are the most important people in the world to me, and I want to see you happy. Both of you." He got up from his seat, came to sit by his wife. With his arm draped around Aretha's shoulders, he smiled. "Let her live her life, Rethie. It's time."

Nona looked on at the exchange between her parents, wondering if her father's words had done anything to sway her mother's views.

After a few long, quiet moments, Aretha spoke. "What are you going to do for work now, Nona?"

"I already talked to the owner of the dance school. I'll start teaching full-time in mid-July." She watched her mother's expression, hopeful that she'd come around.

A deep sigh left Aretha's mouth. "If that's what you want to do, then I suppose I can't stop you. I'm not happy about your decision, though."

Relieved, Nona gave her mother a peck on the cheek. "It's okay, Mommy. We'll agree to disagree on this for now."

Aretha nodded. Seated between her husband and her daughter, she picked up her magazine and returned to where she left off. "You two are something else."

Rising from her seat, Nona gestured to her father. "Daddy, could you come with me in the kitchen for a minute?"

"Sure." Slowly, he slid off the couch and stood.

Once the two of them were alone in the kitchen, Nona went to the fridge for a drink. She turned toward her father with two cans of apple juice. Sliding one across the table to him, she said, "I could use a little advice, Daddy."

"What's your question?" He grabbed the can and popped the top.

"Any ideas on how I can convince Ken that I didn't purposefully betray him?"

His expression turned sympathetic. "You must really be smitten with this man."

"I love him, Daddy."

He smiled. "Well, I better help you. Your mama's still champing at the bit for grandbabies, so let me play my part."

She couldn't help grinning at his dry humor. "Okay, Daddy. What do you suggest?"

"Tell me what's at the root of his secret."

She thought back to their conversations. As she let them replay in her mind, she remembered something he'd said, and it dawned on her. "His father. The whole reason he wanted to keep his family's past out of the article was to protect his father. Hiro Yamada is elderly and infirm, and he didn't want to upset him."

"Sounds honorable. He's a good son." Gordon scratched his chin. "Seems to me the best way to make up with him is to do something that shows respect for his father."

Nona's eyes widened. Leaning across the table, she gave her father a big kiss on the cheek. "Thank you, Daddy. You're a genius."

He leaned back, a satisfied smile on his face. "Well, I like to think so."

Her hope renewed, Nona popped the top on her apple juice and took a long drink. When she left her parents' house, she knew she had work to do.

As soon as she made it back home, she would set her plan in motion. In the end, she was determined to show Ken that she respected his father, that she truly loved him and that she deserved his trust.

With a steaming mug of green tea in hand, Ken sat on the sofa in his father's house. Miyu sat next to him, demurely postured with her legs crossed at the ankles. Across from both of them, Hiro reclined in his favorite chair.

No one seemed to have anything to say. The three of them had been sitting in silence for several minutes, ever since Frances had let Ken and Miyu into the house.

Ken took a sip of his tea, then set the mug down on the black lacquered coffee table.

His father cleared his throat.

Realizing his error, Ken lifted the mug, slid a cork coaster beneath it and set it back down. "Father, you know that Miyu and I came here to talk, not to sit in silence."

Hiro clasped his hands together in his lap. "I understand that."

Ken looked at Miyu, noting how calm she appeared. He was glad she had such a good attitude, but he was starting to get annoyed. "We wanted to speak to you about the article. I know you aren't pleased with what was written."

"No, I'm not pleased. But what can be done about it now? The most painful moment in my past has now been publicized for the world to see." His eyes held a certain sadness as he spoke.

"I'm sorry, Father. I wasn't able to stop this from happening. By the time I found out those details were included, the article had already been published."

"It is as I said. I knew this would happen, from the moment you told me about the reporter." Hiro turned his gaze away, as if looking at some faraway object only he could see. "Aiko betrayed me. I wanted to bury that secret with her. Now…" He shrugged.

Hiro's use of the word *betrayed* hit Ken in the chest like a stone. For a moment, he was speechless. He'd spoken similarly of Nona in reference to the article. Nona had betrayed him, but it wasn't the same thing. As he sat in the room with his father and sister and the specter of his mother's memory, he realized that he'd lived most of his life in the shadow of his father's pain. The weight of Aiko's infidelity had crushed Hiro inside, and he'd passed that shame, mistrust and anger on to his son. It was a tragic legacy, a heavy burden Ken knew he no longer wanted to bear. And in releasing it, he hoped to free his father from the burden, as well.

Miyu broke the silence that had fallen in the room. "If you think it would help to talk about it, we're willing to listen."

Hiro turned wide eyes on Miyu.

Ken reached for her hand. Giving it a gentle squeeze, he nodded. "She's right. You're welcome to say whatever is on your mind to us. Unburden yourself, Father."

He was quiet for a few moments more, with his eyes darting between the two of them. Then he sighed. "There isn't much to say. I worked long hours as county commissioner, sometimes ten or eleven hours a day. Aiko came to me, told me that she was lonely and missed my company. I was so concerned with work that I let it consume me. She reached out to me, and I dismissed her."

Both Miyu and Ken kept silent, out of respect for the older man.

"I blame myself for what happened to Aiko. Had I listened to her, maybe I could have prevented her affair. Then she wouldn't have been in that car with him that terrible, terrible day. He died at the scene, but she lingered on long enough to give birth." His gray eyes welled with tears. "I loved her. I loved her so much. Despite her unfaithfulness, losing her hurt me badly."

When Ken looked at Miyu again, he saw tears standing in her eyes as well.

"And I reminded you of her affair. Of the other man." Miyu sniffled. "I'm so sorry, Hiro."

Ken said nothing, because he sensed something happening between his father and sister. They were both in pain, for different reasons.

Hiro fixed his watery gaze on her. "You were only a child, with no fault in this. I apologize for making you bear the blame, Miyu."

It was the first time Ken had heard his father speak his sister's name. His mother had survived long enough after Miyu's birth to name her, but his father had always referred to her as "the girl" or "her." It was far from a declaration of love, but for Hiro, it was a very big step.

"I accept your apology." Ever gracious, Miyu offered a soft smile.

"I don't know if I can ever accept you as a daughter." Hiro watched her, awaiting her reaction.

"I understand. I'm satisfied to be friends with you, as long as we can put the pain behind us." She rose from her seat on the couch, walking around the table to where he sat. She extended her hand to him.

Hiro took her hand in both of his. Looking up at her, he said, "You have Aiko's eyes."

She squeezed his hand.

Ken watched the exchange and felt a lightness enter his being. It didn't matter to him that it had taken this long. He was simply glad that the two people he loved most seemed to finally be developing a relationship.

As Miyu returned to her seat, Hiro spoke again.

"Ken. Have you spoken to Ms. Gregory?"

He shook his head. "No, not since the day the feature was published."

Hiro scratched his chin. "Then you don't know that she came here to speak to me."

"What?" Ken stared at his father. "When?"

"This morning. She came to the door, and Frances

let her in. She sat just where you are sitting and gave her sincere apology to me for any trouble or strife she caused with her article. You told her of my love of architecture, didn't you?"

"I did."

"She gave me a volume on the architecture of Shinto shrines in Japan. It's beautifully illustrated, very detailed. She presented it humbly and with proper respect."

Ken blinked several times. He had no idea Nona had visited his father. Not only had she apologized in person, but she'd brought a gift she knew his father would enjoy. "What did you say?"

"I accepted her apology. She was very humble and didn't make excuses. She simply asked my forgiveness." Hiro fixed him with a penetrating stare. "But I sense she hasn't yet gained yours."

Ken looked at Miyu, who smiled his way.

"You know what you need to do, Kenny."

He smiled, because he knew what they meant. Whether she knew it or not, Nona had just shown his father that she'd make a wonderful daughter-in-law. She'd demonstrated the one quality a man like Hiro valued most in a wife for his son: humility.

Chapter 19

The interior of Exhibit Hall A of the Charlotte Convention Center buzzed with conversation and activity from the moment Nona stepped inside. It was Ken's big night, the unveiling of his final design for the restoration of the Grand Pearl Theater. Even though she hadn't spoken to him in almost a week, she wanted to be present to congratulate him after his moment in the spotlight.

The occasion had been billed as semiformal, and she'd chosen a strapless maroon peplum cocktail dress. The lace inset in the V neckline kept the dress modest, as did the hemline that stopped a few inches below the knee. She'd paired the dress with a pair of three-inch pumps in metallic gold, and gold earrings hung in her ears. As the chill from the air-conditioning touched her skin, she pulled her gold pashmina wrap close around her shoulders.

She moved through the space, marveling at the size of the crowd in attendance. The one-hundred-thousand-square-foot facility teemed with people, all of whom had dressed in their best cocktail or evening attire for the event. Easels had been set up around the space, displaying concept drawings of the restored building, including the interior rooms and the grounds. She paused to view the drawings, impressed with the visual manifestation of Ken's vision.

She overheard several people speaking about the drawings on display.

"The architect is obviously very gifted," one woman remarked.

The man standing next to her agreed. "Definitely. Look at these designs. The finished product is going to be amazing."

Nona moved past them, a smile touching her lips. She felt proud that the man she loved possessed such talent. Inside, she still felt nervous about what the night would hold. She didn't know if she'd be able to convince Ken that they belonged together, or even that it would be worth his time to speak to her. But no matter the outcome, she had to try. She couldn't spend the rest of her life with him, wondering where he was or who he was with.

Along the east wall of the exhibit hall, a display of items related to Ken's business, Yamada Creative, had been hung on a floating wall. There were large images of the company's logo, as well as photographs and sketches of past design projects. The centerpiece of the display was a series of portraits. One, a company photo, depicted Ken with his assistant and two interns. Another depicted Lynn, sitting on the edge of the reception desk at the Yamada Creative office. But it was the center image that drew her attention. It was the largest picture in the group, and for good reason.

The framed image showed Ken, leaning against his drafting table. He wore a slim-fit black suit, cut perfectly to fit his muscular frame. He'd paired the suit with a crisp, classic white shirt and a solid gold metallic tie. A matching pocket square accented his jacket. His dark hair, neatly parted and combed to one side, just grazed his chin. His large hands were in his pockets, and he wore an intense expression that conveyed his passion for his artwork.

She stood there, slowly shaking her head back and forth. *Damn, he's fine.*

Viewing the image, she struggled to keep it together. This image of him blew her mind. She'd never seen him dressed like that; the closest she'd come was seeing him onstage with the band. That night, all the guys had been dressed alike. But seeing him like this, in such a well-tailored suit, with no one else to distract from his utter gorgeousness…she could barely process it. She sucked in a breath and swiped her fingertips over her chin, proud of the fact she'd managed not to drool.

Logically, she knew he'd simply been looking at the camera when the image was taken. Emotionally, though, she felt he was staring at her, into her. It was as if he were looking directly into her very soul. She remembered feeling the same way the night they'd first made love, when he looked into her eyes. She'd felt as if the core of her being, as well as her body, were laid bare before him in that moment.

When she finally tore her eyes away from the image, she continued to walk through the exhibit hall until she reached the area that had been set up for the audience to hear the evening's speakers. Padded chairs had been set up in rows, all facing a large stage. A podium centered the stage, backed by a group of five chairs.

Many of the chairs were already occupied, as the speakers were due to take the stage within the next half hour. She strolled down the center aisle, checking either side for an empty seat. Her preference was to be as close to the stage as possible. *If Ken is dressed tonight the way he was in the photo, I need to see up close.*

Though she wasn't here in any official capacity, she approached the front of the seating area, where the first row had been marked off for the press. Taking the last empty seat directly behind the row where the press would be seated, she tucked her small handbag into her lap.

A few minutes later, Nona saw a group of people approaching the stage. As they began to step up on the stage, she saw the familiar face of Mayor Tyson, as well as the three committee members she'd interviewed for her feature. Ken's assistant, Lynn, was also present.

The last person to step onstage was Ken. When she saw him, her jaw dropped.

He wore the exact same outfit from the photograph. And though she'd thought it impossible, he looked even more delectable in person. She drew in a deep breath, letting her gaze follow his movements as he took a seat onstage.

As the event began in earnest, an emcee gave a brief welcome before introducing Ken. "And now, please welcome our architect, Ken Yamada of Yamada Creative."

Ken approached the podium to the sound of enthusiastic applause. Resting his open palms atop the wooden surface, he looked out over the audience. "Thank you all very much for coming out tonight. I'll do my best not to bore you." His eyes swept the room until they landed squarely on Nona's face.

Her breath caught in her throat as they made eye contact for the first time since the night he'd stormed out of that dressing room at the Blue Lounge. She waited, unsure of what would come next.

A ghost of a smile touched his face, and he winked at her.

Feeling her nervousness melt away, she let a small smile show through. His gesture gave her hope that when this was over, he'd hear her out.

As he spoke, his gaze traveled the room. Every few minutes, though, his eyes would find their way back to her face. "I feel very fortunate to have been chosen to restore the Grand Pearl Theater. I've completed a number of projects around the southeastern United States, but this is the first time I'm completing a renovation of a historic site. I'm excited to move forward with this project and to see the finished product."

Nona smiled. The passion he had for his work was evident in his words, his tone, his expression. She couldn't think of anyone who would be better to restore the Grand Pearl.

"This building has so much historical significance, not only to Charlotte and to Mecklenburg County, but to this region and this nation. At one time, during segregation, it was the only theater African Americans in the area could attend. By bringing my vision for the theater to life, I hope we can start a process of healing and reconciliation for the misdeeds and injustices of the past. I also hope that we can look toward a brighter future for our city, one of tolerance, togetherness and love."

Applause filled the room as Ken finished his speech. People jumped to their feet, Nona included, to express their approval of his words. She locked eyes with Ken, hoping her expression conveyed how much she'd been moved by his words—and how much she'd missed him.

The minute Ken finished shaking hands and exchanging pleasantries with the city officials, he left the stage to find Nona. He'd been watching her throughout his speech, and she knew it, because she'd been just as focused on him. Now that his obligations for the evening were complete, he wanted to speak with her.

She'd been sitting in the second row during his speech, but as people got up from their seats and started moving en masse toward the exits, he'd lost sight of her. Now on the exhibit hall floor, he sidestepped between bodies, excusing himself every time he bumped against someone. His gaze swept the room, seeking the dark beauty in the gorgeous deep red dress.

Over the next few minutes, the crowd thinned out

considerably as people left the venue. A small number
of stragglers remained, chatting in various corners of
the room, but the exhibit floor had mainly emptied.

When he finally caught sight of Nona, he stopped
in his tracks. She stood with his father and Miyu, chatting near the floating wall with the company display.
He wasn't close enough to make out their words, but
all three of them were smiling, and he considered that
a good sign.

Miyu noticed him first. "Great speech, Kenny."

Hiro's expression conveyed his agreement. "I'm very
proud of you, son."

"Thank you, Father. Miyu." He looked between them
to where Nona stood.

"Ken." She said his name in a voice that barely surpassed a whisper. Her eyes met his, and the rest of the
world seemed to fall away.

Miyu sensed what was passing between them. She
linked arms with Hiro. "Come on. Let's take a look at
some of the drawings."

Hiro didn't protest as Miyu led him away.

Ken took a step in Nona's direction, entering her personal space. "My father told me that you stopped by."

"I wanted to apologize. Even though this was all a
horrible mistake, I'm still responsible for what happened." She blinked, her dark lashes fluttering.

"He knows you were genuine, and because of the
way you approached him, you've really endeared yourself to him." He reached for her hand, capturing it in
both of his. "And to me."

She trembled, tears gathering in her eyes. "Ken, I'm

so sorry. You have to know that I would never purpose-fully betray you."

"I know that now." He drew her body close to his, reveling in the feeling of her soft, warm form filling his arms.

As she slid her arms around his neck, her explanation tumbled out in a rush. "I'd written about it in my journal, and I didn't even realize I'd taken my journal to work. The intern grabbed it when he came to get my article revisions, and then my boss—"

He placed his index finger against her lips. "It's okay, honey. I get it."

"Really?" Her voice held a touch of fear, as if she were afraid his forgiveness would be snatched away at any moment.

He curled his finger beneath her chin, lifting her face up. For a moment, he simply stared at her, taking in the beauty of her dark, almond-shaped eyes, high cheekbones and the soft fullness of her red lips. "Nona. I forgive you. In a way, I owe you a debt of gratitude."

Confusion made her brow crinkle. "What? Why would you say that?"

"Look at the two of them." He gestured behind her, to where his father and sister were. They stood together, looking at one of the concept drawings he'd created for the event. "Ever since she was born, he's been keeping her at arm's length, never really developing a relationship with her. This is the first time they've ever spent a significant amount of time together."

Nona glanced over her shoulder at them. Turning

back to him, she shook her head. "I'm happy they're getting along, but I can't take the credit for that."

"Yes, actually, you can." He brushed his fingertips over her jawline. "Your article was the catalyst for all this. It made my father uncomfortable enough to finally sit down and talk to Miyu, and to address his feelings about what happened with our mother. So, thank you, Nona. Thank you for helping me put the broken pieces of my family back together."

She smiled as a tear coursed down her cheek. "I'm glad I could help."

"Besides, I need to apologize to you."

"For what?"

"For being so stubborn and secretive. I should have just been open with you from the beginning." He pushed a fallen lock of her hair away from her face. "I realize I was broadcasting my issues of mistrust onto you. I made you work way too hard to learn who I am."

She shrugged. "You did. But I'm glad I went through it. You're more than worth the effort it took."

He felt a smile stretching his lips. Having her in his arms again made him feel lit from within, as if his heart were smiling, too.

"So are you and I back on good terms now? Because I miss you."

He nodded. Leaning in, he said, "We are on better terms than ever. And I missed you, too." He brushed his lips against hers. It was a brief, teasing kiss meant to convey his growing desire. "Now let's go to my place and I'll show you how much."

She purred low in her throat. "You don't have to ask me twice."

To reward her, he leaned down and kissed her again.

Chapter 20

Back at Ken's house, Nona struggled to think clearly as the two of them kissed and fumbled their way into the house. By the time they reached the hallway that led to his dining room, she'd given up on that. All she wanted was to get undressed and let him do whatever wicked things he dared.

He pressed her back against the wall in the hallway, his large hands stroking her shoulders and arms as he kissed her deeply. She wound her arms around his neck, letting the intensity of the kiss sweep her away. Soon she felt as if she were melting from the inside out. The core of her femininity felt like molten lava: hot, wet and threatening to run down her thighs at any moment.

Breaking the kiss, she pointed toward the sliding doors that led to his deck.

"Out there?" His hands continued to tour her body as he posed the question.

"Yes…" Her reply came on the heels of a sigh as he started tugging at the neckline of her dress.

"In a minute." He tugged the dress down enough to expose one breast. Cupping his hand around it, he lifted it. A moment later, his warm mouth covered her nipple.

"Oh!" A bolt of pleasure shot through her as he flicked his tongue over her hardened flesh. The initial sound melted in a series of short, high-pitched moans as he continued to pleasure her. She let him have his way, arching her back as her body begged for more of his magic.

He drew away, and she saw him smile in the dark. Then he grabbed her hand, as if to lead her through the dining room.

She was so ripe with need, her legs had turned to jelly, and she faltered.

Sensing her instability, he placed one arm around her shoulders and the other beneath the backs of her knees. Lifting her into his arms, he carried her through the dining room and unlatched the sliding door. Opening it, he took her outside onto the deck.

The warm, humid air flowed over her exposed skin, sending another charge of pleasure radiating from her damp, exposed nipple and throughout her body. She trembled in his arms, closing her eyes. He stopped walking but continued to cradle her in his arms, sprinkling kisses over her eyelids, her cheeks, her jawline and the column of her throat. Gently, he set her down.

When she came to rest atop something soft, she opened her eyes to see where she was.

He'd placed her on the cushion of his chaise lounge. From her vantage point, she had a wonderful view of his garden. The bright red leaves of his Japanese maple trees, as well as the green plants growing throughout the yard, were lit with solar lighting. She could also see the bench nestled within the plants, where he'd brought her to orgasm the first time they'd made love. She'd been mesmerized by the beauty of his garden that night, and tonight was no different. It was a beautiful setting for them to share their most intimate moments.

She sat up on the chaise with her legs draped over one side. He joined her, taking a seat on the end of the lounge. He lifted her feet and placed them in his lap. Then he removed her shoes, carefully undoing the ankle straps before slipping them off and placing them on the deck floor. While she watched him through hooded eyes, he eased his hands up her bare legs. She lifted her hips and hiked up her dress, not caring whether she wrinkled it. His warm palms grazed her inner thighs, and he applied the slightest pressure there. "Open for me, honey."

She did as he asked, and in the next moment, she felt his questing fingertips between her thighs. She gasped, her head dropping back on the cushion as he boldly pushed her panties aside and found her center. She was slick with desire, and he used that to his advantage as he plied her. His touch, gentle yet insistent, drove her to the brink of madness. Her back arched as he slid two fingers inside her, stroking, teasing.

"So sweet." He whispered the words in the darkness. "So perfect."

She uttered a series of sharp cries, which soon lengthened into long, throaty moans as he took her higher and higher, closer to completion. Fire seemed to spread through her body, sparked and stoked by his skillful hands. It spread from between her thighs, the glow expanding until it reached the very tips of her toes and fingers, and when it could expand no farther, she came, crying out his name.

He eased his hand away, allowing her a moment to recover a few of the scattered fragments of her sanity. When she opened her eyes, she saw him stripping off his jacket. In a matter of minutes, he'd tossed it aside, along with his shoes, shirt and trousers. His hardness strained against his boxer briefs, and her hungry eyes took in the sight of him releasing his member from the fabric and rolling on a condom.

When he rejoined her on the lounger, she shifted positions so that he was beneath her.

He smiled as she straddled him, placing his hands on her hips to guide her.

She needed no assistance finding what she wanted most. A moment later, she took him in, savoring the sensation of his hard length as it filled her. She ground her hips, loving the way his eyes rolled back as she began her ride.

Before the night ended, she planned to make up for every second they'd spent apart. Leaning forward, she gripped his shoulders, tossed her head back and let the motions of her body carry them both away to paradise.

* * *

Ken stood with his hands on his hips, observing Nona's motions. They were alone in the kendo room at Satori Martial Arts on the first Saturday in August, and night was falling on the Queen City. While he looked on, she held her bamboo sword and demonstrated the movements he'd taught her over the past several weeks. It was something of a pop quiz to allow him to evaluate her grasp of kendo.

She completed her demonstration and returned to first stance. "How did I do, baby?"

He smiled, genuinely pleased with her progress. "Honey, that was amazing. You've shown so much growth in your technique these past few weeks."

She tucked her sword beneath her arm, padding over to give him a peck on the cheek. "That's because I have the best damn private tutor a girl could ask for."

"You're right. I can't deny it." He winked.

She burst into peals of laughter. "You're an absolute mess, you know that?"

"And yet you love me anyway."

Her free hand cupped his jaw. "Yes, I do. More than anything." She followed her words by placing a sweet kiss on his lips.

Before they'd come to the studio, he'd fed her strawberry shortcake. Now he tasted the remnants of the rich cream and tart berries that lingered in her mouth. The sweetness of the kiss made it difficult for him to control his urges. He eased her away. "If we keep that up, the people practicing in the next room are going to get a free show."

She grinned. "You're probably right." Taking a few steps back, she put a bit of distance between them. "So what now?"

He looked around the space, remembering the first night he'd invited her here. In the space of a couple of months, she'd gone from a nervous woman who'd never done martial arts to someone with excellent command of a *bokuto*. In the same amount of time, she'd gone from a stranger to the love of his life. He never could have imagined the way things played out between them, and he wouldn't change it for the world. "Now, we fit you for your *keikogi* and *hakama*."

Her brow hitched. "My what and my huh?"

He chuckled. "Your jacket and trousers, honey. This fashionable outfit I'm wearing. The other intermediate kendo students wear it as well."

She looked down at her clothing, a T-shirt and a pair of sweatpants she'd cut off to make shorts. "You mean I can't keep practicing in my sweats?"

"Not if you want to continue training."

"May I ask why I can't just wear my sweats?"

"That was okay when you were first starting out. But kendo etiquette dictates that students who have passed the beginning level wear the proper attire."

She nodded, executed a bow. "As you wish, Sensei."

He bowed to her, unable to hide the smile on his face. He'd kept their private lessons casual, not holding her to most of the etiquette rules the official students of the dojo practiced. "You've been paying attention. That will come in handy if you want to begin training in earnest."

She looked thoughtful for a minute. "I think I do. I really enjoy doing this."

"You'll have another sensei, though. Our relationship means I can't properly instruct you, especially as you become more advanced."

"I understand." If she was disappointed, she didn't let on.

"The day will come when I'll expect you to spar with me." He started walking toward the bench, where they'd left their bags.

"Oh, really."

"Yes, really. And if I win—" he paused, turning her way "—I win your hand in marriage."

Her smile was soft, loving. "What makes you think you'd have to do all that to get me to marry you?"

He pulled her into his arms. "You know how I love a challenge."

She giggled. "That's great, because I love being a challenge."

As he drew her in for his kiss, he hoped she'd never, ever change. "I love you, Nona."

"I love you."

Their lips met a breath later, and he heard her *bokuto* clatter to the floor.

Neither of them cared.

When he broke the kiss, he slipped his hand inside his jacket. Pulling out the small box he'd placed there earlier, he dropped to one knee on the polished wood floor.

Shock registered on her face. "What are you doing, Ken?"

"You know what I'm doing, and for once, don't challenge me." He opened the box, revealing the glistening heart-shaped diamond ring he'd custom designed for her. "Nona, will you marry me?"

Tears sprang to her eyes, and she covered her sob with her hand.

"Is that a yes?" He looked up at her expectantly.

Nodding, she dropped to her knees in front of him and let him slip the ring onto her finger.

And when she fell into his embrace and turned her face up toward his kiss, he felt he'd claimed a prize far greater than he could have ever imagined.

Epilogue

On a starlit evening in early September, Nona ex-
changed vows with Ken. Nona wore a shimmering,
champagne colored knee-length sheath, made of satin.
Her hair hung in loose curls around her shoulder, held
back on one side by a crystal embellished clip. Ken wore
a cream suit, crisp red shirt and cream tie, and the unmistakable smile of a man about to marry the love of
his life. As they stood beneath a tall stand of pine in
Freedom Park, where he'd first kissed her, they shared
their first kiss as husband and wife.

As the ceremony ended, Nona walked hand in hand
with her husband to the area where a simple reception
had been set up for them. Champagne, finger foods
and cupcakes were all artfully arranged on two picnic

tables, and Nona watched as their friends and family ate and mingled.

Ken left her side momentarily, returning with two champagne filled flutes. Handing one to her, he smiled. "Here you go, Mrs. Yamada."

She accepted the flute, returning his smile. "I love the way that sounds." The two of them eased into the side-by-side armchairs that had been set up for them to hold court in.

"So do I." He placed a soft kiss on her forehead.

Darius approached then, with a beautifully wrapped oblong box in his hand. Passing the box to Ken, he spoke. "This was on the gift table, man."

Confused, Nona said, "Why did you bring it over? We haven't started opening gifts yet."

"Look at the tag." Darius gestured, then strolled away.

Ken lifted the box and read the tag. "It's from the Music Man."

Nona's eyes widened. She'd heard about this mysterious figure, who seemed to be well-informed on all the band members' lives, but chose to never reveal his identity. "Well, open it. I want to see what it is."

Ken tugged off the ribbon, then stripped away the wrapping paper. An envelope fell out, landing on Nona's lap as Ken stared at the clear box.

"Oh, my God. They're Max Roach's drumsticks, engraved and everything." Ken turned the box over in his hands a few times, staring in awe at the two wooden sticks inside.

Opening the envelope, Nona carefully unfolded the letter inside, then read it aloud.

Ken,
I hope you enjoy the sticks. I'm not going to tell you who I am, because it's not important. I will say that I'm an old friend of Joseph Franklin's. My main aim in what I've been doing has been to encourage you and the rest of the Gents to continue pursuing your art. The world needs your talents, that much is clear. And the reason I've waited for all of you to marry is simple: love is the greatest inspiration any artist can ever hope for. May every day for the rest of your life be filled with that inspiration.
-The Music Man

Refolding the letter, she tucked it back into the envelope and passed it back to her husband. "We're never going to know who he is, are we?"

Ken shook his head, slipping the envelope into an inner pocket of his sport coat. "Probably not. Now that we're all married, I think his job is done."

She had to agree. Looking into his eyes, she asked, "Do you think being married will change your music?"

He draped his arm around her waist, pulling her close. "I don't know, but if it does, it will definitely be for the better."

He kissed her lips, and she didn't have any other care.

* * * * *

Donovan emptied the last of his drink. "You know what's
funny?"

"What?" Chloe asked, finally turning to fully face him.

Chloe blinked and Donovan could have sworn time
slackened to slow motion. She fixed her doe eyes directly
on him.

"We've known each other since we were kids, attended
the same schools and lived within the same social circles for
years and there's still a lot I don't know about you."

"You're right," Chloe acknowledged.

"We should do something about that." His desire flew
past his lips before he had a chance to filter the thought.

Chloe cleared her throat.

KPEXP0617

"How about dinner tomorrow night?" *Why waste time?* Donovan thought. He wanted to learn more about Chloe Chandler and he had no intentions of toying with his interest. "I know a beautiful place on the other side of the island."

"That should be fine." Chloe looked at her watch and then looked toward the resort's entrance. "Let me check with Jewel and make sure—"

"Just you and me," Donovan interjected.

"Oh…" Chloe's surprise and coyness made him smile once gain.

"I'm sure Jewel wouldn't mind but do check with her to make sure. I wouldn't want her to feel left out." The fact that Jewel had never returned from her "bathroom" run wasn't lost on him. Jewel was rooting for him and he was sure that she was intentionally giving them space.

"I'll do that." Chloe looked at the door again before sitting back.

"It's been a while. I don't think she's coming back," Donovan responded to Chloe's constant looking back toward the hotel.

"Maybe I should go check on her. She did have quite a few of those rum cocktails."

Donovan stood. "Come on." He held his hand out. "I'll walk you to your suite."

Chloe looked at him for a moment before taking his outstretched hand. A quick current shot through him when their palms touched. Donovan liked it. He wondered if she felt it, too, and if she did, had she enjoyed it as much as he had?

*Don't miss IT STARTED IN PARADISE
by Nicki Night, available July 2017
wherever Harlequin® Kimani Romance™
books and ebooks are sold.*

Get 2 Free Books,

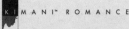

Plus 2 Free Gifts—

just for trying the
Reader Service!

KROM17R

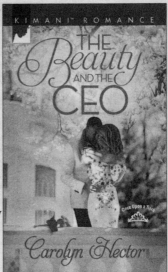